The
Problim
Children

ISLAND
IN THE STARS

The Problim Children

ISLAND IN THE STARS

NATALIE LLOYD

INTERIOR ILLUSTRATIONS BY
DAVIDE ORTU

KATHERINE TEGEN BOOKS
An Imprint of HarperCollinsPublishers

Katherine Tegen Books is an imprint of HarperCollins Publishers.

The Problim Children: Island in the Stars
Text copyright © 2020 by HarperCollins Publishers
Illustrations copyright © 2020 by Davide Ortu
www.harpercollinschildrens.com

ISBN 978-0-06-242827-1

Typography by Andrea Vandergrift
20 21 22 23 24   PC/LSCH   10 9 8 7 6 5 4 3 2 1
❖
First Edition

FOR CONNOR DUKES,
because he is brave, curious, and kind–
a true adventurer.

Mona Problim

Monday's child
is fair of face,

Toot Problim

Tuesday's child
is full of grace,

Wendell Problim

Wednesday's child
is full of woe,

Thursday's child
has far to go,

Thea Problim

Friday's child is
loving and giving,

Frida Problim

Saturday's child works
hard for a living,

Sal Problim

Sundae Problim

But the child who's born
on the Sabbath day is
good and wise in every way.

—Anonymous

Prologue

Once upon a Saturday, a small boy stood at the helm of a pirate ship. The sea stretched out all around him—silver, endless, and chopped into sparkling waves by a playful wind. The sun was shining, but the boy did not feel warm. He didn't even feel excited, the way most children would if they got to ride on a boat this size. He didn't feel much of anything.

Until now, he had always loved danger. But that's because danger had always been on his side. He'd come through many terrifying adventures, some with bruises, some with scrapes, but always with great stories to tell. This time, however, the plan hadn't worked like he'd thought it would. Now his family was even more fractured than it had been before. Somewhere out on that distant, shining sea, the boy's little brother was trapped. Waiting and hoping to be rescued.

There was a villain out there too. Maybe several

1

villains, for all the boy knew. There would be storms and starlight and some terrible crossings—all perilous. All risky. Dangerous. What if danger betrayed him?

What if he lost everything?

Doesn't matter, thought the boy. I made a promise. I'll see it through.

As the pirate ship disappeared over the horizon, a mechanical squirrel flicked its tail from the shore. The squirrel's heart beat a *ticktock* inside its metal chest. It waited until the boat was so far gone that it looked like a speck at the edge of the world. Then the squirrel ran.

Everything was in place now.

The villains and heroes were on a path to crash into each other, shooting stars on a sky-colored sea. The squirrel couldn't control the outcome. But it had made a promise too. To help. And it would try. Especially now.

This was, after all, the beginning of the end.

1

Sal at Sea

"**S**AL!" Mona yelled, shaking him out of his thoughts. Thank goodness.

It wasn't like he had time to feel sorry for himself. He had way bigger problems—and Problems—to focus on.

Like rescuing poor Toot.

Like somehow getting rid of Cheese Breath, the gross old villain who'd kidnapped him. Not to mention Ari, Cheese Breath's rotten accomplice. (Sal had actually thought she was a true friend before she betrayed him.)

Like finding a fountain that maybe gave eternal life and was also possibly evil.

Like driving this old pirate ship. Which was much more complicated than Sal had assumed. Sunlight had been smeared across the sky when they'd first borrowed the ship this morning. By noon, storm clouds had filled every corner of Sal's view. Now, a few hours later, the sea rolled choppy and dark. It was *perfect* weather, in other words. But a bit challenging for boat driving.

"What's your deal?" Sal asked, glancing at Mona. "I'm trying to steer."

Mona's dark hair blew in slashes across her face. She looked like a pirate. Or like a ghost that would haunt a pirate ship, maybe. She pointed to the horizon. Lightning beamed and bolted, highlighting a terrible storm blocking their path.

"Just trying to get your attention so you don't drive us into a hurricane," Mona said. She paused, and a sly smile stretched across her face. "Or *doooo*. I've never been inside one before."

"It's only a little summer storm," Sal informed her, as wind roared across the boat. "Plus, this is the fastest path to the barrier islands. If we go around the storm, we'll waste time. Rescuing Toot is the priority. And Mama. And probably Papa too, at this point. Then we have to smash the fountain. It's a busy day."

"The sky looks really angry," Thea Problem said, as she scampered over beside Mona and scanned the horizon. Sal watched Thea's hand tremble as she gripped the rail of the ship. "Should we go back to Lost Cove to get help?"

"F-from who?" Wendell, Thea's twin, came to stand beside her. He rested a hand on her shoulder. "*W-we* are the help. We're the h-heroes this time."

Sal watched Thea stand up straighter, like she was blooming at the sound of her twin brother's words. *Words are like seeds,* Mama Problem had told him once. *Plant them and people grow.* He'd seen it proven true time and time again. Of course, saying nice stuff like that came naturally to Wendell. Less so to Sal. Thea had become very brave over the past few weeks, since the Problems had moved to Lost Cove. She was still fearful, sometimes. But a wild new courage had hatched in her soul. It didn't take a scientist to see.

"We should at least get belowdecks," Thea said. "So we don't fall over the side." The helm, where Sal and some of his siblings currently stood, was on the upper deck of the ship. The lower deck and the librarian's office were a few steps down. Belowdecks is where the books—which were most likely soaked—were all shelved.

"I can't go below," Sal reminded her. "I have to steer the ship!"

He wasn't about to ask for help on something this important. Mama Problim had also urged him to trust people: himself, his siblings, the friends he'd make. Based on his present situation, this advice was wrong. Sal Problim could only ever trust himself.

"Then how will we stay planted in the storm?" Thea asked.

Plants. Perfect! Sal knew the answer already. Plants were almost always the answer.

"Make sure everyone's wearing a life vest," Sal said. "And stay calm. I have a plan." Grudgingly, he added, "Wendell, could you take the wheel for a few minutes?"

"I will take it," Mona cooed.

To which everyone yelled: "NO."

Instead, Wendell jumped to the helm. Wendell's element was water. If anybody could drive them to safety, it would be him. Sal jogged down the slippery steps to the lower-level deck, bursting through a faded red door to an office. At some point—before this boat became the Lost Cove Library—this office must have belonged to the head pirate. But there were no pirates in sight today. Just a bunch of kids and piles of books.

Seated at the table (beneath a light swinging like a pendulum) was Sundae Problim, who held an *ork-ing* pig named Ichabod (the family's beloved pet). Alex Wong, Sundae's crush, sat next to her. Or was Alex actually her boyfriend? (So weird that Sundae had a *boyfriend*.) Beside Alex sat Violet O'Pinion, the brilliant girl next door, whom they'd just found out was also their cousin. (He hadn't quite had time to process that reality yet.) *Violet was his cousin.* One thing was certain, Sal knew: this was already the most eventful summer in Problim family history.

Violet studied a map spread out in front of her, mumbling to herself and sending little puffs of breath across the bubble helmet she always wore because of her allergy to air. Biscuit, Violet's dog, was cuddled in her arms. Sal noticed Biscuit's eyes scanning the map too, as if the dog could also read. (Maybe she could, Sal reasoned. Dogs were amazing creatures. He'd make a note of this discovery later.)

"Violet," Sal said, resting his hands on the table.

The gardening tools that were always attached to his jacket jingled as he leaned. "Do you have any Wrangling Ivy with you?"

"Always," Violet said, looking at him as if this was a ridiculous question. She pulled a jar from her backpack and tossed it to him. Holes were poked in the lid of the jar, just the way he'd shown her. Perfect, he thought.

Ivy swirled around inside like octopus arms. Sal loosened the lid and dumped the plant onto the table. The ivy stretched each tentacle as if waking up from a long nap. And then it began to crawl. And grow.

Quickly.

2

One in a Million Stars

"WHOA, no!" Alex yelled. He tried to push away from the table but accidentally flopped his chair over backward instead, slamming against the boards with a thump. Sal rolled his eyes. Why were people so afraid of plants?

"It's okay, Alexander the Great!" Sundae said, as she helped him back up. "Plants love to stretch and move and grow."

"Why is it trying to eat me?" Alex yelled as a thin, green tendril tightened around his ankle.

"It's protecting you," Sal said, a bit too harshly.

In a softer voice, Violet said, "It'll hold on to all of us so we don't—"

The ship lurched, suddenly, groaning as it tilted so far left the table began to slide.

"—go overboard," Violet finished. A pile of books fell loose from the shelf in the corner of the room, clattering against the floor.

Sal nodded. "Right. Keep your life vests secure. Make sure the ivy's got you. It's going to get rough out here."

"Oh, how fun!" Sundae said. "Just think—this could have been a peaceful, steady boat ride, but now it will be exciting!"

"I might need a bucket," Alex said sheepishly.

"What's all this, Violet?" Sal asked, as Sundae pushed past him to find a barf container.

"Maps of all the barrier islands," Violet told him. "The known ones, anyway."

"There are so many. It's going to take us forever to find the right one."

Sal's neck prickled. The Problims only had one clue: they were headed to a place where the stars fell into the sea. *That* was the place where they would finally find the treasure they'd been seeking: the dangerous, and secret, location of the final fountain of youth. More importantly, that was where they would find Mama and Baby Toot . . . since their kidnapper, Cheese Breath, was also headed there. As for Papa Problim, well, he'd also left to find Mama. So ideally, he would be there too. But the biggest question remained unanswered: Where was this mysterious island?

Violet nodded. "Where the stars fall into the sea . . . none of the islands have starry names, of course. So, I'm not sure what that clue means. Just that it's one of them."

"It's okay," Sal told her. "Grandpa always comes through. If he hasn't given us the clue already, he will."

Violet gave him a sad look. "How, Sal? Unless he knows we're out here, how can he send any more clues?"

Maybe he does know, Sal thought. That thought— that little spark of hope—had bobbed around like a buoy in Sal's heart since the day they imploded the bungalow. What if Grandpa was still out there somewhere? Still alive? What if they'd *all* be together again soon? Not just Mama, Papa, Toot, and the rest of them—but everyone Sal missed?

"Sal!" Thea shouted from up above. "Get back up here! Quick!"

"I'll be back when the storm's done," Sal said,

holding the door open for the ivy to slither through. The plant wriggled through the opening and up the wet stairs, across the upper deck to the helm. It slithered around the ankles of Thea, Wendell, and Mona.

"You can always count on Wrangling Ivy," Sal yelled, jogging up the steps toward them. He felt a thin vine of ivy snake around his wrist. "You might fly off the ship for a second, but it will always snatch you back!"

"Like magic," Thea said, as the ivy knotted itself around the ship's mast.

"Science is magic," Sal informed her.

He staggered as he reached for the wheel. The ship seesawed across the ocean. A mighty groan and the boat curved hard to the right. Waves were climbing higher, he noticed—licking at the sides of the ship like some huge, hungry sea monster. Water splashed along the upper deck, filling his shoes. And making the steering wheel very slippery. Thunder bellowed.

So did Thea.

"Where's the fox?" she yelled, squinting against a cold torrent of rain.

"AHOY!" Frida shouted from the crow's nest.

"Fear not my siblings,
A storm shall brew.
But with courage and luck,
We'll all pass through!
If not . . ."

Thunder crashed overhead again, this time with such a violent *BANG* that Sal let go of the steering wheel to cover his ears.

". . . it's been nice knowing you," the fox shouted, finishing her rhyme.

Thea's breath came in short bursts. "You guys. Look. The lightning . . . the lightning bolts . . . they look . . . they look like—"

"Don't say it," Mona shouted.

"SEVENS!" Thea shouted.

BOOM, yelled the thunder. An unruly wave bounced the boat, making the boards feel like a trampoline.

"Nobody panic," Sal reminded them.

"Who's panicking?" Mona asked. "This is wonderful!"

Sal gritted his teeth, bracing wet sneakers against the slippery boards as he tried to keep the wheel from spinning again.

"We'll never make it," Thea said.

"We will," Sal assured her. "We're all strong together."

They *would* do this.

He *would* protect them.

They had a mission to complete. And he had a promise to keep.

"Um . . . Sal . . ." Thea's voice faded into a fearful little sigh.

Reluctantly, Sal glanced at her face . . . and then in the direction of her gaze. Up. And up. A wall of water—the mightiest wave he'd ever seen—was rising above them. Billowing. Churning.

"Oh, wonderful," Mona said, a purr in her voice. "Now we can have some fun."

Calm in the Chaos

"**S**-STEADY!" Wendell shouted. The boat began to climb the dark hill of water. Sea spray peppered their faces, making them squint.

Sal's fingers hurt from gripping the wheel so hard. Ocean waves sloshed over the sides of the boat, tossing Mona over the edge. But the ivy snagged her, yo-yoing her back into place. Waves curled up around the boat like monster tongues, like some plant for which Sal had no name.

Thea grabbed her twin brother's arm. "Wendell! You can control water. Right?" Each of the Problim children was born on a specific day of the week. And each day of the week was connected to some strange elemental power. Wendell, for example, was connected to water.

Wendell shook his head. "A l-little. B-but I c-can't control a whole s-storm without T-Toot here. W-we have to w-work t-together. It works best that way."

"Just the six of us might be enough to make it calmer, at least," Thea suggested. She yelled for Frida the Fox, and they all stood (and hunched and sometimes slid) together. Side by side, hands locked inside one another's.

"Sal," Thea called his name. She held out her hand. "Let's try to calm the water. Like we did at the carnival."

"Great idea!" Sal said. At the carnival last night, they'd all held hands and the weather had gone haywire. The seven of them were all connected to the earth or the atmosphere in a powerful way. They could make it reveal treasures when they were together. Could they also make a storm like this calm down? It was a fine experiment.

Sal turned the wheel loose. He grabbed Thea's hand.

"How do we do it?" Mona shouted.

"Think of Wendell," Sal yelled, "while Wendell thinks of the ocean. Maybe if we think of him—of all the things about him that are strong and awesome . . ."

Wendell—who clearly did *not* feel strong or awesome at this second—gave his brother a grateful nod before he closed his eyes. His siblings did the same.

The boat groaned as if it was exhausted, unable to take one more tumble. Sal slid. But Mona's hand latched around his arm, yanking him back into position. She clenched his hand and he closed his eyes. He thought of Wendell—his little brother—smart and strong and capable of anything.

"You've got this," Sal mumbled. "You can calm the ocean, Wendell! Easy."

And . . . Wendell did. When the Problems opened their eyes, the skies were swirling from black to silver. The ocean was still angry. But the ship wasn't heaving now. The darkest clouds were floating away, a long, dark cape dancing to some other place in the sea.

Finally, slowly, the Problems let go of each other. Sal's hand ached from holding theirs so tightly. Sundae, Alex, Violet (plus Biscuit, who was secured to her chest), and Ichabod staggered out of the office to join them as they celebrated the end of the storm.

"That was easy enough," Sal said, pushing his

wet hair out of his eyes. "Storm at sea? No problem for a Problim! We should reach the first barrier island by morning. And somehow . . . we'll figure out which one has to do with stars. We'll get Toot back. We'll destroy the fountain."

"Shhh!" Violet said suddenly, cuddling her wet dog close to her chest. "Do you hear that? It sounds like something down beneath us?"

"Maybe some books were knocked loose during the storm?" Sal asked.

"Or m-maybe it's the g-ghost of this library sh-ship," Wendell offered. He didn't say this like he was afraid. Just matter-of-fact. "R-rumor is that this sh-ship is haunted."

"Just when I thought the fun was over," Mona said happily.

If it's a ghost, it's a noisy one, Sal thought. Clunky footsteps sloshed belowdecks. The sound moved toward the stairs. And then, it began to climb. It wasn't a very big ghost, Sal reasoned. The footfalls were light. But surely little ghosts were just as dangerous as big ones.

Thunk.

Thunk.

Thunk.

Sal felt the hair on his neck rise.

What if it was Cheese Breath? No, the steps were too small. Desdemona? Ari? (Ugh. Just the thought of her made him feel sick. And then it made him feel angry.) What if this was some new villain they hadn't even met yet?

"Get behind me!" they all shouted at once, trying to protect each other.

The Problim children stood close, ready to lock hands if they needed to. Ready to launch this visitor—human or otherwise—back to Lost Cove.

"Is this how all our dates will be?" Alex mumbled to Sundae. (Sal heard this and rolled his eyes.)

Biscuit, still secure in Violet's arms, snarled at the bolted door.

Thunk.

Thunk.

With a slow, steady creak, the door opened.

Sal tensed his muscles to keep from trembling at the sight of the terrible villain in front of them.

4

The Secret in the Ship

"**L**ook how cute!" Sundae cried.

"I hate cats," Sal said through clenched teeth.

Sal studied the visage of the terrible beast standing in the doorway. It looked like a fuzzy, orange bowling ball with large, green eyes and a bristly tail. Fact: it was the most rotund cat he'd ever seen, twenty pounds at least. A long streamer full of paper stars was wrapped around the cat's back paw—debris from the storm they'd just weathered. A thin paperback book was tangled in the streamer too. Which was probably what Sal had heard clonking up the steps.

Also, the cat was wearing a shirt.

"Who puts a shirt on a cat?" Sal asked.

Sundae picked up the cat, cuddling it against her chest, untangling its paws from the streamer. The creature purred. And Sal was able to see the shirt also had a message:

KING CAT!

What did that even mean?

"He was reading *Bunnicula*," Sundae declared, untangling the book from the streamer.

(Sal did not dispute this finding. It was further proof that animals could read. Even cats. Cats had terrified him since he was little. They always looked like they were plotting things. Mona would be a cat if she were an animal.)

"Th-that c-cat belongs to M-Miriam Sanch-chez," Wendell said in a hushed, nearly worshipful tone. "She's the t-town librarian. She had g-gone home for the n-night when we b-borrowed the b-boat."

It had not occurred to Sal or—clearly—any of his siblings that the town librarian's cat might be asleep somewhere in the library when they borrowed it. He hadn't felt so bad about borrowing a library—it was basically the same as borrowing a book, right? They'd return it. But a cat? That felt a lot like stealing.

"Do you think she'll be mad that we borrowed the boat?" Sal asked. "And the cat?"

"I d-don't think so," Wendell said. "She r-reads. All r-readers know that r-real life is w-weirder than fiction."

"We will take wonderful care of King Cat," Sundae said, kissing the top of his head. "Perhaps he can show me around downstairs. Or maybe he'll help us once we reach the island."

"H-has anybody w-wondered," Wendell asked softly, "Wh-what we'll d-do if we can't find the *r-right* island once we g-get there? Assuming we actually g-get there a-at all?"

"Or," Thea said. Her voice was a raspy waver. She twisted her hands nervously, as if she didn't want to speak the next part aloud. "What if Desdemona finds us before we find them?"

"She won't," Sal assured her. And he remembered again—a calm morning about a year ago, back in the swampy trees. The day he'd made an important promise. He shook his head, trying to make the memory skedaddle. It made him sad, and he didn't have time to be sad right now. "Seven together—we can find any treasure. We will always find each other."

"And when you do that, and you find this island, your plan is just to smash something, right?" Alex reasoned. He'd kneeled down beside Ichabod to pet him. Poor Ichabod, Sal realized, was not the same without Toot.

"Yes," Sal said. "Grandpa's clue said: *destroy it.* The fountain is evil."

"Is it really though?" Mona asked softly. "I mean, people are evil. Can a fountain be evil?"

"Yes," Sal nearly shouted. "If Grandpa believed it, then I believe it. Now we only need to figure out the place where the stars fall into the sea. Then we'll help Grandpa finish all of this."

Alex nodded. "Must be cool to be a Problim."

"It is," Violet said proudly. She beamed at Sal. Violet was still reeling, and rejoicing, from the discovery that she was family. "It changes everything. I just wish I could help more. . . ."

Mona sighed and looked down at her watch. A watch Sal didn't remember her wearing before. "Alas," Mona said. "It is time."

Fear rippled through Sal's body. "Time for what?"

"Three," Mona said softly, closing her eyes. "Two . . . one . . ." Eyes wide open now, she looked to the sky.

"What did you just do?" Sal asked.

"TALLY HO!" the fox shrieked from the crow's nest (Sal hadn't even seen Frida climb back up there).

"Look aloft,
There she flies!
A strange golden cannonball
with bright, beady eyes!
TAKE COVERRRRRRRRR!!!"

Eye of the
Sparkly Sparrow

As Sal turned to look up at the fox, Thea screamed his name. "WATCH OUT!"

The Wrangling Ivy snagged Sal's ankle, yanking him to the ground, just as something small—and heavy—smashed into the ship.

"Is it a cannonball?" Sundae shouted excitedly. "Are we under attack?! What fun!"

Sal shook off the ivy and leaned down to look at the fresh dent.

The offending cannonball was golden—as Frida had described it. But it wasn't really a cannonball at all. It was a bird—a mechanical one—with shiny metal feathers and sparkly red eyes. Small gadgets whirred along its chest. It reminded Sal of the little mechanical squirrel that had shown up on Kaboom Day. The one Grandpa had clearly sent to give them clues and help them find their way. (Where is that little squirrel? Sal wondered.) Sal used his tools to dig the bird out of the dent in the ship. Then he carefully propped it upright.

"Are you okay?" Thea asked the tiny creature.

The bird didn't budge. Or blink.

Ichabod waddled closer to sniff. Nothing.

Sundae crouched down near the bird and began whistling. "I'm welcoming it to our boat," she explained to Alex.

Thea leaned in closer to Sal. "It's got to be one of Grandpa's creations, right? Maybe it has a message for us!"

Violet looked at Sal and smiled.

But Sal looked at Mona. "Did you make that happen?" he asked softly. "Are there things you aren't telling me? Where did you get that watch?"

Mona pulled away before he could take her watch. "Even siblings have secrets, Sal Problim."

She turned away without offering any further explanation. What secret was Mona hiding?

What secrets were the rest of his siblings hiding?

Hours later, twilight had snuggled close around the library ship. The storms had rolled back like a curtain, leaving peachy-pink skies overhead. Still, the mysterious bird offered no explanations. The Problems—plus a couple of friends, plus a pig and a bird—all gathered in a circle on the upper deck of the boat.

"There's s-so much s-sky out here," Wendell said, his face turned up. "It's b-beautiful."

Sal humored his brother and looked up too. The wishing star pegged the corner of the sky. Other stars twinkled awake as he watched. He remembered years ago, carrying Toot outside in the swampy woods on a starry night. He'd wanted to tell him true things: about the speed of light and supernovas and dwarf stars. But Toot pressed his tiny hand to Sal's mouth, *shhh*. He had just wanted to see. To be amazed, for a minute or two. And then he'd tooted[1] and they went back inside.

Sal's arms hurt at this memory. It had been nearly

---

1 **#2**: The Hangry Puff: A warning Toot fires to remind his family that if he doesn't eat soon his mood will quickly sour. Smells like takeout food forgotten in a car overnight.

a full day since the last time he'd held his brother. And all because he'd trusted Ari O'Leary.

"Let's try to focus," Sal said. "I want to see what we have so far. Everybody put the clues in the middle."

The goods were as follows:

- One water witch—aka a very long, enchanted tree branch—ideal for finding fountains of youth. Wendell was the family witcher, so he kept it with him (or near him) at all times.
- One vial of water (he assumed), which Mona had discovered in the Pirates' Caverns of Lost Cove.

"What I didn't notice in the caverns," Mona said, "is that there's this tiny tag tied around the bottle with instructions. It reads: "Truth Teller Drops 2.0. A true adventurer's best tool! To be used on any artifact, human or otherwise, that won't spill the beans."

"Interesting," Sal mused.

"And here's a sketch of the islands," Violet said, pushing her notebook to the center. Grandpa's last clue had included a map, just a cluster of specific islands off the coast. The last fountain, he believed, was somewhere there: "the place where the stars fall into the sea."

"And now we have this," Mona said, tapping the mechanical bird with her shoe.

"We have one other thing," Sundae said softly to Sal. "I'll share it at the end of this meeting, though."

Sal's interest was on high alert. Why not just share it now? Why did his siblings suddenly have so many secrets?! Before he could ask, Thea shouted: "OH!"

They all stared at her.

"Remember how we sang to the squirrel?" she asked. "That's what we should do to the bird too. See if it's a clue. Maybe that's how it opens."

"L-let's t-try!" Wendell shouted.

All together, they sang the lullaby their mama had sung to them back in the Swampy Woods. Sal joined in, even though he loathed family sing-alongs.

Monday's child is fair of face,
Tuesday's child is full of grace,
Wednesday's child is full of woe,
Thursday's child has far to go,
Friday's child is loving and giving,
Saturday's child works hard for a living,

But the child who's born on the Sabbath day
is good and wise in every way.
Adventure waits—for good—forever—
to a perfect seven who work together.

The bird's eyes begin to whir. The Problems looked up at the billowing sail, expecting Grandpa's face to show up there—some kind of filmed clue like all the others.

But that is not what happened.

This time, the bird spit something out of its beak. Something that looked like a tiny scroll.

Sal unrolled the scroll and scanned the page, eyes widening at what he saw. "It's a letter from Grandpa!" He began to read:

DARLING DREAMERS,

YOU ARE SO CLOSE TO FINDING—AND DESTROYING—THE TERRIBLE TREASURE AHEAD OF YOU. A WARNING: I HAVE MADE THE WAY COMPLICATED SO THAT THE TREASURE DOESN'T FALL INTO THE WRONG HANDS. YOU MUST ALL WORK TOGETHER TO FIND—AND FINISH—THIS LAST QUEST.

HEREIN LIE YOUR DIRECTIONS:

WEDNESDAY,

THE WITCH,

IT MUST BE COMPLETE.

IT WILL HELP YOU GET TO THE TREASURE.

(THOUGH YOU'LL ONLY EVER FIND IT TOGETHER.)

THURSDAY,

SET SAIL

TO SWEET ST. MARIA,

WHERE JEREMIAH JUICE IS YOUR AID.

(TRUST EACH OTHER! GO QUICKLY! BE BRAVE!)

MONDAY,

MAKE YOUR WAY

THROUGH THE MISERABLE MIST.

(THE MONSTERS WILL BECKON, BUT YOU MUST RESIST!)

FRIDAY, SATURDAY, AND DEAR SUNDAE TOO—

AN ISLAND OF STARS MUST BE CONQUERED BY YOU.

TOGETHER IS THE WAY TO REACH THE RIGHT END,

WHERE A RABBIT-SHAPED CAVE CALLS YOU TO DESCEND.

(HERE NOW, THE ENEMY MUST BE YOUR FRIEND.

FIND AN O'PINION AND DO MAKE AMENDS.)

(AND FRIDAY—LISTEN CLOSELY—
YOUR GIFT MIGHT TAKE TIME.
BUT THE LOVE OF YOUR FAMILY
GIVES YOU REASON TO SHINE.)

NOW SEVEN AT LAST,
SEVEN AS ONE,
CALL UP THE WATERS,
BLOCK OUT THE SUN,
SMASH THE LAST FOUNTAIN,
FOR NOW AND FOREVER.
DESTROY IT, DEAR CHILDREN,
AND DO IT TOGETHER.

AND SAL, DO REMEMBER,
WHEN THINGS SEEM TOO HARD,
EYES TO THE SKY
AND L

The last letter stretched into a long slash of a pen mark, as if Grandpa had stopped writing suddenly.

Sal's eyes scanned the page frantically, trying to find something else. Anything else. But there was nothing. He flipped the page . . . nothing.

"Well?" Mona asked. "Go on."

"It just trails off," Sal said. Now that hopeful, bouncy feeling he'd had when he found the letter was being squished out by anger. "It ends midsentence. Like he didn't get to finish it. What was he going to say?!"

"Please don't get upset," Thea said softly. "Maybe we'll figure it out later!"

Sal swallowed down the horrible feeling of worry in his throat. "But why didn't he finish it? Doesn't that worry you?"

"I prefer to focus on what's giving me joy right now," Mona said, clasping her hands together. "For one, I am thrilled to be on a boat with all of you. It's a shame we're in a hurry. There are so many things I could do to you out here where we are isolated. Here where no one can hear you scream."

"That's the spirit, Mona!" Sundae cheered.

"Second," Mona continued, smoothing her skirt. "We've already finished two parts of the new riddle. Wendell, the stick is finished. The water witch will lead us where we need to go once we get there. Also—making amends with an O'Pinion? We've done that thanks to Violet. And her little mongrel dog."

Biscuit snarled at Mona as she continued: "So,

we're up to the Thursday part of the clue. . . ."

"I'm Thursday's child," Thea chirped.

"And you're good with directions," Sal said. "So once we get to the island in the clue—"

"The Isle of St. Maria," Mona said matter-of-factly. "Everybody knows what that is. It's the most visited barrier island. There's a little town there full of beachy, touristy things. We go there. And somehow Thea leads us to someone called Jeremiah Juice."

Thea shook her head. She giggled nervously. "I don't know who that is. Or what that is."

Sal held up the scroll. "But you can find them. Don't doubt yourself."

"You're right," Thea said softly. She bounced up suddenly.

"Where are you going?" Violet asked.

"I'm going to try the internet again," Thea said. "I might as well start with a search on Jeremiah Juice, right?"

"P-perfect!" Wendell shouted. "I'll g-go with y-you."

"Me too," Violet said. And the three of them disappeared belowdecks. Frida, in a blur of orange, followed.

"Sal . . . Mona." Sundae's whisper held a warning. "Remember, I wanted to show you all one more thing. I didn't want to show you in front of Thea . . . she'll only worry. But we're not just in a hurry. We have a deadline."

6

The Deadline

The stars had all come out to watch as Sundae pulled another letter from the pocket of her jeans.

"I found this attached to Ichabod's collar when we came out of the Pirates' Caverns," Sundae said. Sal was surprised by the tremble in his big sister's voice. Usually Sundae was endlessly hopeful and happy about every discovery. Even awful ones. "After Cheese Breath took Tootykins, he must have left this for us."

Sundae's hand shook as she passed it along to Sal. Mona glanced over his shoulder to read it along with him.

This note was very short, the writing scratchy and scrawled. This was a warning, not a riddle:

Dear Problim children,

I will meet you in the Harbor of DuVerney on Wednesday afternoon. At that time, I expect you to lead me to the fountain. Once you do, your brother will be returned to you. Do not be late. Do not plan anything sudden or strange. This can all be very easy, if you choose. Toot and Mommy send their regards.

Sincerely,
Augustus Snide

"Cheese Breath," Sal said, pushing his hand through his hair. He spun to lean against the rail and stare out at the starry horizon, the place where the black water touched the night sky. So inky, Sal thought. So . . . endless. And somewhere, on that endless sea, Toot was waiting for them. And to get him back they had to find this one fountain—on one of these islands—in two days.

"I'm worried about him," Sal heard himself say. He didn't like to show fear. He needed to instill confidence in his siblings, but . . . Toot was a baby. There were no words big enough to describe how much Sal hated himself for losing Toot. Keeping his family together was his responsibility. And he had failed.

"You're the one who trusted that strange girl," Mona said, as if she could read his mind. Sal flinched.

"Mo," Sundae cautioned. "You, of all people, should understand how gutsy it is to trust someone. It's not Sal's fault that someone he trusted let him down. Like Sal said, we'll find him."

Sal closed his eyes and breathed in the ocean smells: salty anchovies, warm bananas . . . a #9²?!

Sal's eyes blinked open. "Do you smell that?!"

Mona and Sundae took deep breaths. Then gagged a little. And then they smiled.

"It's him," Sundae said. "He's letting us know he's out there!"

2 #9: The Come-and-Find-Me: Smells like salty anchovies and warm bananas. A toot emitted by Toot Problem when he is bored playing hide-and-seek and prefers a snack instead.

"He's okay," Sal said, his voice filled with hope.

"For now," Mona added. "As long as we find him by Wednesday."

"Hang in there, Toot," Sal said. "We're coming. I promise."

Where Villains (and Smells) Abound

Arianna O'Leary had wrapped a handkerchief around her nose. Even on the top deck of the old man's rickety ship—where sea air was usually clean and wonderful—the stench was ripe. But she wouldn't let Toot Problim go—not for anything. She didn't want him to get hurt, for starters. But more importantly, she'd made a promise to Sal Problim. And even if Sal didn't want to be her friend ever again—totally understandable, considering she was involved in this kidnapping fiasco—she would keep her promise. She'd been a bad friend to him. But he had been a wonderful friend to her.

Wooooomp.[3] She felt a vibration against her leg, where the baby sat, and she turned her face away. "I was going to say maybe we should find a way to let your siblings know you're safe. But that's what you're doing, isn't it? It's working, for sure. Every boat in the ocean should be able to smell that one."

The baby beamed. He was very proud of himself. To her surprise, Toot Problim hadn't cried even once since he'd come aboard the ship as a captive. Instead, he'd sat adorably resolute, bow tie straight, chin up like a proud little king. But Toot's cuteness was deceiving. Anytime the old man got in close proximity, Toot became a tiny, snarling monster. Ari thought Toot would hate her too. But he didn't.

Not at all.

Once the old man had gone belowdecks for the night, Ari sat down to cry for what she'd done, still holding Toot in her arms. She liked the warm weight of him. He was comforting, somehow. She'd learned to cry quietly over the years—she did not want the old man to hear. But after a few soft sobs, she felt

3 **#35**: The Fart of the Four Winds: The flatulent rally of a true adventure. Contains bold notes of dead fish in the ocean and chicken litter in a wide-open field.

Toot's tiny hand patting her arm. *He* was comforting *her*. Terrible-awful-friend-betraying *her*.

It made no sense. She'd done something terrible. She'd taken the baby from his family. Ari knew she had no choice but to help the old man. And yet . . . she had never known how much she wanted a friend until she met Sal Problim. At first, she'd told the old man that she was spying—watching the enemy in his natural habitat. But really, after a while, she wanted to get to know Sal. And she wanted to know his family. Seven all together (she'd only ever counted six, but that was just a detail). Sadness and jealousy seesawed in her heart when she watched them play.

Jealousy because Sal had so much family to hang out with.

To play with.

To do things with.

Sadness because she didn't.

Jealousy because there was so much love in Sal's life.

Sadness . . . because, well . . . facts are facts.

And the fact was, there would never be love like that for Ari.

She didn't have a big family. Or even a medium family. She had no family.

No mom to tuck her in at night. No dad to read stories with her.

No siblings to launch her into the woods on a catapult.

The old man reminded her of this all the time (as if she could ever forget). He reminded her of other things too: That she was unlovable. Unwanted. Unnecessary. A simple thief. A stupid girl.

Toot patted her arm, as if he could read her mind. Then he farted.[4]

"Gaw," Ari said, pressing her handkerchief to her nose. Sal had told her that Toot had hundreds of farts—the Problim children had cataloged and named them. This was how he communicated. "You've got to learn to talk," she told the toddler. "The toot thing won't be cute much longer. Definitely not once you start school. Can you say any words at all?"

Toot smirked. He probably could, Ari reasoned. He just didn't want to yet.

Suddenly Toot's eyes squinted, and he glared over Ari's shoulder. The old man was climbing the rickety

---

4 #82: The Comforter: Smells of dog breath and a well-worn sneaker. Intended to feel like a hug, though it permeates the air with stink.

steps from belowdecks. Ari held the baby close as she turned to face him. The door creaked open, and the old man's shadowy, slumped figure filled the space.

"That baby stinks," he bellowed. "I can't get any sleep for the smell."

Toot smiled, dimple-deep. And giggled.

"So sorry *you're* inconvenienced," Ari drawled.

"Be careful with your attitude, dear." The old man's voice rattled around in his chest like it didn't quite fit there anymore. Like it had become detached long ago. "I keep your secrets, you get me to my treasure. . . . That's how it works. As for little Toot, we can only hope his siblings come on Wednesday. I've got no use for a baby on my boat. He'll have a new nickname if he stays here too long. Shark Bait, perhaps?"

Toot growled, narrowing his eyes. The old man slammed the door and went back down below.

Ari sighed and hugged the baby close. "I won't let him hurt you. They'll be there on time, and then we can all go home."

Or he would, at least. Ari didn't have a home of her own. She'd go wherever the wind carried her next. It will be an adventure—that's what she tried to tell her heart. But her heart wanted something more. Maybe a place . . . or maybe people . . . who felt like home to her.

Toot clapped his hands. And tooted twice.[5]

Ari groaned, pressing the handkerchief to her nose. "Gaw, I wish I understood what you were trying to say. How about we try a bedtime story?"

Toot nuzzled against her chest. Ari leaned against the deck, looked up at the stars, and did what she'd done so many nights in her life: she told stories. She imagined she was somewhere else. She slipped into the safety of her imagination. She hoped for a future that she knew, deep down, would never be hers.

Just off the shore of Lost Cove, a small yacht cut a white scar across the surface of the night ocean.

"That way!" shouted Desdemona O'Pinion. She stood in the front of the vessel, while her brother, Joffkins, drove as fast as the boat would go.

"TURN!" she shouted.

Joffkins obeyed, veering so hard to the left that the boat tilted, and the occupants nearly slid out of their seats. Carly-Rue O'Pinion let out a soft squeal

---

5 **#6: The Paul Revere:** A trumpetous fart of warning. One toot if by land. Two toots if by sea. Smells of cruciferous vegetables.

as she slid across the seat. Her brother, Will, grabbed the straps of her life jacket just before she thumped onto the floor.

"Thanks," Carly-Rue mumbled. Sometimes, Will was obnoxious. But in times of distress, he was a fine big brother.

"Easy on the gas, dude," Will said. "Violet's a smart girl. She's fine."

"Go back to your game, darling Will," Desdemona said. And then, in a whisper: "Nobody wants your opinion."

"I care about your opinion," Carly-Rue said to him softly. Will nodded his thanks. And then he slipped his CosmicMorpho Mask back over his eyes.

Carly-Rue cleared her throat. "How do you know where to find them, Mom?"

"I smell the little one," Desdemona said with a hiss in her voice. "They'll all be trying to find him. If I find him first, I'll find them all. Don't worry, dearest. I have a plan in place."

"Huh," Carly-Rue reasoned. "I thought that smell was dead fish. Glad you're prepared. Plans are important." She stole a glance at her big brother. Will tapped his chin twice—a signal they'd worked out quickly before leaving the carnival.

Because they also had a plan in place.

Carly-Rue breathed a sigh of relief and straightened her pageant crown. "I bet Violet is leading them. She's really smart."

"I can't believe they've stolen my girl!" Joffkins O'Pinion shouted, his voice rattling with rage. "My sweet, innocent Violet. They'll pay for this. We'll send them to homes for troubled children across the world. They're a real threat, those kids."

(They really weren't, Carly-Rue knew.)

As if her mom even cared about Violet, Carly-Rue thought. Desdemona only cared about any of this because the Problims were after something that Desdemona wanted. Carly-Rue didn't know what that something was. Only that it turned her mom into a beast of a person.

"Violet went on her own, you know," Carly-Rue informed them. "She wanted to go with them. Nobody forced her to do anything."

Desdemona glared at her. "How do you know she wanted to go?"

Carly-Rue felt her heart drop. "She told me."

"And you didn't tell me?"

"No."

No—because somehow Carly-Rue knew, deep

in her gut, that her mother was wrong about the Problim children. Disagreeing with her mother on this was the right thing, which made no sense at first. Carly-Rue had always assumed her mom was right about everything. That adults could always be trusted because they'd learned enough to never make mistakes. But she didn't believe that now.

Desdemona plotted on as the boat roared ahead, making empty threats about Carly-Rue being grounded from her phone. (Carly-Rue could not let that happen. She had to have her phone . . . for *reasons*.) Will patted Carly-Rue's shoulder in solidarity.

"Leave the girl alone," came a rumbly, old voice behind her. Carly-Rue turned to look at her grandfather, Stanley O'Pinion, and smiled. There are people in the world whose words feel like a hug, and Grandpa Stan was one of them for her. But he'd been very quiet so far on this trip.

"Don't tell me how to parent," Desdemona fired back at him.

"This was too far, Desdemona," Grandpa Stan offered, firm but gentle too. "You don't know what you've done, inviting that man back into town."

"I'm taking back what's ours!" Desdemona finished. "Just like you've always wanted."

Stan said nothing to this. He simply turned his face to the sea.

"Oh, now you're silent," Desdemona said. And she leveled her father with a glare so icy, Carly-Rue and Will ducked down further in their seats.

Carly-Rue slipped her phone out of her dress pocket.

She's so mad. IDK if this will work.

A second later the screen flickered in response:

LeeLee101: We're here for you, girl. She won't hurt the PRBZ.

BamaLlama: Team CdT's in place. It's all good.

Sk8Punk: Bring us snacks l8r?

Carly-Rue grinned, and typed:

I'll try. Just stay QUIET.

Then she quickly tucked the phone back into her pocket so her mom wouldn't see it. Because if Desdemona saw the texts, she might go downstairs and realize three stowaways were hidden below: LeeLee, Noah, and Alabama. The Problims had helped them all, in some way. Carly-Rue thought maybe the Problims needed help now. So she'd rallied the best soldiers she could find (one of whom was still wearing sequins). Rescue was on the way . . . thanks to the reigning corn dog princess.

Carly-Rue adjusted the sparkling crown pinned atop her curly hair and smirked.

8

Finding Jeremiah

On Monday morning, the Lost Cove Library rolled into the misty harbor of the first barrier island: the Isle of St. Maria.

Alex and Ichabod steered the ship into the harbor. And the Problim children, plus Violet, huddled down below in the ship's hull—the actual library—researching the layout of the town. Somehow (and Sal didn't quite know how), Wendell and Thea had found internet access in the middle of the ocean. King Cat slept on top of the monitor; his fluffy orange tail draped down over the screen. Sundae held the mechanical bird in her arms.

"Just a fun fact about this island," said Thea, as

the Problims gathered around her, "there are no cars here. People only ride bikes or walk."

"That's a relief," Violet said softly. She whispered to Sal: "If Aunt Desdemona gets here, we'll be able to see her, maybe. Have time to get away." And then Violet looked down sadly and bit her lip. "I'm sure my dad is coming with her. I know he'll be mad at me."

Sal reached out and gave Violet's shoulder two solid pats. He wasn't good at physical contact. But this seemed like a comforting gesture. "What about Jeremiah Juice, Thea? Any info on that name?"

"J-just a quick m-mention," Wendell said, poking furiously at the computer keys. His search results beamed onto the screen, reflecting off his glasses. "H-here." Wendell gently pushed the cat's tail away.

Sal leaned close to the screen and read the words aloud:

THE ISLAND GAZETTE

March 18, 1965

On Friday night, the harbor of St. Maria was strung with lights as tourists flocked from miles around to hear popular songbird Jeremiah Juice. Though

Miss Juice's only publicity is word of mouth, the folk singer draws a mighty crowd—of humans and animals alike. It is said that Miss Juice can hit notes so high, the rainbow canaries leave their nests to come and listen. Miss Juice is most often seen at The Sweet Ralphie Tegen, but don't be surprised to find her suddenly appearing in a living room, on a street corner, or standing on a table in the piazza as well . . .

"*Miss* Juice," Thea repeated. "I assumed Jeremiah Juice was a man."

"A-and this," Wendell said, cutting her off and clicking another open tab.

LETTER TO THE EDITOR

October 18, 1974

Dear Editor,

Years ago, my husband and I first visited the Isle of St. Maria to hear the beautiful music of local legend Jeremiah Juice. For a while, we were able to find out about her secret concerts. And then, they just stopped! Upon our recent visit to the island, we were sad to hear no one had seen—or heard of—Jeremiah Juice in years. It's as if she vanished as mysteriously as she once appeared. Where did she go?!

"L-looks l-like she s-stopped singing all t-together," Wendell said. "H-ow do we kn-know if she's even h-here now?"

"Because Grandpa said she was," Thea said. "I believe him. I say we start by finding this place where she liked to play at the most. The Sweet Ralphie Tegen. Scoot over, Wendell. . . ."

Thea clicky-typed and—*slowly*—results began to creep up on the screen.

"Ugh, so this is tricky too," Thea said. "The Sweet Ralphie Tegen is a hotel. Or . . . it was one. It's hard to find, apparently. It says the pure of heart know when they've arrived."

"Does that mean we can't take Mona?" Sal asked. (Mona punched his arm hard.)

Thea chewed on her lip, scrolling the page for any other clue. But there wasn't one.

"Hey," Sal nudged her. "Don't doubt yourself. If Grandpa thought you could do this . . . then you can. You can find anything, Thea. This is your moment."

Thea bloomed at this compliment: her shoulders

rolled back and a smile lit her face. Planting a seed and watching it bloom. That was part of the promise he'd made. Don't be scared, he told himself. We'll find this Jeremiah Juice, and she'll get us to the island in the stars.

"Problims, pile up," Sal said. "Let's get going! This will be easy."

Sal was delighted to see his siblings scrambling out of the library hull, excited for the mission ahead. He was far less excited when King Cat jumped down from the computer and stared at him. For far too long. As if he knew things. As if he too had secrets. King Cat stretched, then waddled out the door after the children.

The Isle of St. Maria

The rising sun had floated higher in the sky as the Problim children prepared to disembark. Already, it was Monday morning. Sal's heartbeat felt like a clock ticking in his chest. Two days. So little time for such a big mission.

"The sun looks like a warm orange egg yolk cracking over the horizon," Sundae said. "GLORY! And Sal! That color is smashing on you!"

He'd slid a yellow parka over his tool-jacket, even though it wasn't raining. "Just trying not to draw too much attention," he said. "We need to find the hotel—talk to Jeremiah—and head to the island with the fountain. Fast. We've only got two days."

Mona smirked. "You're doing a wonderful job of blending in. Wearing bright yellow. Your tools will still make noise. Just leave the stupid tool-jacket on the boat."

"No," Sal nearly shouted as he scrambled down the ramp. "I have to have it. It's not like your flytrap. It actually serves a purpose."

Mona narrowed her eyes. "Leave Fiona out of this. She's belowdecks actually doing something useful."

"Please don't fight," Thea begged.

Mona rolled her eyes and walked down the ramp next, followed by Wendell.

"Ichabod will stay here with Alex and me, to guard the ship," Sundae said from above them. "And we'll take care of the little bird too."

Sal watched as Violet walked to the edge of the ramp and paused. She held Biscuit against her chest, over her heart. Like a small, fuzzy shield.

"I can't help but draw attention," Violet said nervously. "Should I wait here too?"

"Definitely not," Sal told her. "Unless you want to, I mean. Don't you want to explore? My tools make people nervous, is all. Your mask isn't like that."

"But it's different," Violet said softly. "People always stare at whatever looks different."

Sal tried to think of something encouraging to say, but the words weren't there. Probably because he knew Violet was right.

Violet didn't move. She stared at the ramp leading down to the dock as if it were a magical bridge leading to some bright new world. And . . . it kind of was for her. It was for all of them. None of them had been this far from home before, but Violet hadn't thought she would ever get to leave home at all.

"I've always dreamed about adventure." Her voice was breathy against the mask. "But it's a little different when it's right in front of you, isn't it? When all you have to do is take another step?"

She looks so small without her wings, Sal thought. Maybe the wings had given her courage. How could he plant a seed of courage for Violet . . . ?

"We'll be with you the whole time," Sal said. "We won't let anything happen to you."

This made Violet smile, just a little. His heart warmed at the sight of it.

Then, with the smallest sigh—just a crackle through the speakers of her mask—Violet stepped onto the ramp. She made her way down to Sal, slowly, stepping onto the dock with a low, steadying breath.

Frida pounced onto the dock beside her.

"Off we go!
Adventure awaits!
Let's find Jeremiah and do what it takes!"

"Lead the way, Thea," Sal said.

With a deep breath, Thea stepped in front of her siblings. Wendell took his place beside her, adjusting the water witch—which he kept strapped to his back like a fishing rod. He liked to keep it close in case they needed it. And so no one could steal it without him knowing.

"I don't like this place," Mona said with a groan. "It's disgustingly beautiful."

The Isle of St. Maria rolled out and up in front of them, a series of gently waving hills dotted with pastel-colored houses. The roads ahead were made entirely of stone, with the occasional dandelion shooting through the cracks. Seagulls swooped lazily through the sky. Flowers bloomed from boxes in the windows. Statues of people dancing were dotted all along the shore. And on the side of an old brick building up ahead was a faded mural: an advertisement for a bottled drink called Bloomfizz.

"That's a Wishbloom!" Sal said, running up to the mural.

"A what?" Mona asked.

The old advertisement showed a little girl floating above the ground, beaming, lifting her glass bottle high in the air. On the ground beside her was white flower, painted in such a way that it glittered when the sun shimmered across it.

Sal lifted his parka and fished around in his pocket until he found a tiny vial. He held it up for his siblings to see. "Wishblooms," he said. "I've been studying these flowers. They have a rare kind of magic."

A wonderful kind of magic.

Sal felt a lump of sadness rising in his throat.

Because he remembered the day he first discovered a Wishbloom. It was the last day he'd seen Mama Problim. The day he'd made two promises: to keep his siblings together, and plant a seed of possibility instead of being critical. And to trust them, and himself, to bloom. Am I failing at both? he wondered.

"Hold on to this," Mama had told him, pressing

the flower into his palm. "The last wish is the most magical of them all."

That's not why he'd kept it, of course. He didn't think it really granted wishes. He just kept it to study. Or something.

"Sal?" Mona said. "Tell us what you're thinking."

He shook his head. "Not important." He slipped the Wishbloom back into his pocket.

"Have you heard of this drink?" Violet asked.

"We r-read about it," Wendell informed her.

Thea filled in the info: "Bloomfizz was a drink manufactured before people realized those flowers were so rare. When people drank it, they could run in the air for a few minutes. At like, twice the speed of normal running."

Mona sighed in delight. "Can you imagine what I could do with a bottle of Bloomfizz?"

The children looked at each other, horror sparkling in their eyes. They could absolutely imagine it. Thank goodness it was gone now.

Sal couldn't wait to tell Mama all about it. He couldn't wait to see her again.

"Let's get going," Sal said. "Let's find the hotel."

Thea led her siblings down the street, curving past a church, a flower stand, and shops just opening for the day. Stomachs growled in a rumbling chorus as they smelled the baked sugar of the waffle stand on the corner.

"I think I'm too obvious," Violet said.

People *were* staring at her, Sal knew. He'd seen them. Little kids especially were pointing. Little kids were always so pointy.

"Just pretend you belong here," Mona said. "Walk like you know where you're going."

"Even though none of us knows where we're going," Sal said, as Thea mumbled something to herself, paused, and then cut down a shadowed alleyway.

"What's she doing?" Sal whispered to Violet and Mona.

"Listening to her heart," Violet said matter-of-factly. "Finding her way."

"Finding the way would be much more fun if we didn't have a deadline," Thea said. "And if Toot were here."

"These riddles are slowing things down," Sal said.

"They're helping us," Mona told him. "Imagine if Cheese Breath simply had directions he could

follow! That old bone-bag's not smart enough to figure riddles out. We are."

Violet cleared her throat. "Seriously guys, should
I go back to the boat?"

"N-no way," Wendell told her. "W-we need
y-you."

Sal glanced toward the sidewalk where two old
ladies were eating salads. They'd paused, forks lifted
toward their mouths, to watch the children pass.
Their lettuce blew over the street like green-leafy
confetti.

"Who eats salad for breakfast?" Sal asked.

Just as Violet breathed out a soft: "I shouldn't
have come."

Sal paused now, and so did everyone else. He
hated to see the sadness in her eyes. So he took off
his parka and folded it into his arms. Now his tools
were shiny and visible, gleaming in the morning
light.

"Now they can stare at both of us," Sal said.

"That's cool of you," Violet said. "To be weird
with me."

"We're family," Sal reminded her.

She smiled. And she walked beside him, with her
chin lifted high and Biscuit tucked against her chest.

"I would rather fit in with all of you than fit in with anybody else," Violet said. She stood taller now. Walked with a near-skip in every step. "Weird is our kind of normal, and I like it."

Sal offered a smile. He understood that. The Problim children were like puzzle pieces—a jumble of funny edges and wild colors and all together, they fit just fine. By most standards, they were weird. To him, they were wonderful.

The streets were becoming more crowded, full of conversation and jingly bicycle bells. Wendell pulled Thea out of the path of a lady on a bike who was late for work. A cluster of pink flower petals blew across Violet's mask (Biscuit managed to eat one). Thea grabbed Wendell's arm just as he was about to zombie walk into an adorable corner bookshop. And again, when he saw the cupcakery around the corner.

"Focus," Sal said to his brother. "We can be tourists another day. This time, we've got Toot and Mama and Papa waiting for us."

Thea continued down a shadowed alleyway. "According to the map—and my heart—the hotel is . . . just ahead. I think."

They jogged farther down the street, their sneakers

squeaking on the stones. The sides of buildings, once visible, were now covered with kudzu. Through the vines, Sal noticed old newspaper ads selling Patsy Cline records, fresh caramel corn, and roses for a cent.

"It probably looked very different years ago when Jeremiah was here," Thea reasoned, a little breathless. As they rounded the corner, Sal caught a whiff of garbage which made him feel 1.) exhilarated (the dump!) and 2.) lonesome (Toot . . .). Stinky smells made him think of his baby brother, and he missed him so badly. And lately thinking of Toot also made him angry . . . because he thought of Ari.

Reasons Ari Was the Worst Villain of All:
1. They had met at the dump (she'd invaded his sanctuary!)
2. He'd helped her find banjo bees (she'd used him!)
3. She'd pretended to be his friend (the worst offense by far!)

Sal felt stupid, and he felt duped. He should never, ever have trusted her. Clearly, he couldn't trust anyone who wasn't family. And even that was hard considering Mona was part of his family. . . .

"Here!" Thea shouted, jumping to a stop in the middle of the narrow street.

The Problims spun around, looking . . . but saw nothing except kudzu-covered brick walls and a silver garbage can. King Cat had followed them. He lounged on top of the tin trash can lid, studying the Problims intently. Sal watched as the cat's tail curved into a question mark.

"Somewhere there's a hidden door!" Frida shouted excitedly.

"Is it there in the wall?
Or down on the floor?
What wonders might we have in store?"

"Did you just hear something?" Violet asked softly.

"Something besides Frida?" Sal answered, as his little sister—the fox—scampered around to begin her search.

Violet looked confused. Her mouth twisted, just a little, like she was trying to decide whether or not she should say what she was thinking. She must have decided against it, because she said, "Never mind."

"Where are you going, fox?" Mona yelled. Now Frida was climbing the ivy, singing a song:

"I'll follow the birds
to old Jeremiah.
If I don't find her here,
I'll simply climb higher!"

Violet whispered gently to Sal, "Remind me to ask you something later. About . . . *Frida*?"

What about Frida? he wondered. She'd said his sister's name like it was a question. But he didn't have time for that now. He kept his eye on the fox until she stopped.

Waited.

And pointed . . . up.

Up.

Settled in a long, fluffy line across the rooftop sat a row of rainbow-colored birds. They were pastel like the houses on the shore—pinks and blues and yellows, with beady eyes and golden beaks.

"It's got to be here," Thea said happily. "And Jeremiah must be here too. The birds loved her. Remember?"

Sal took his shears from his sleeve and cut away

curtains of ivy until he found an old, black-metal sign:

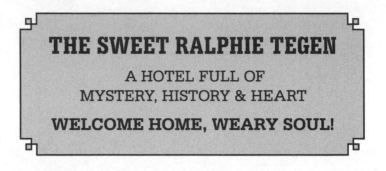

THE SWEET RALPHIE TEGEN

A HOTEL FULL OF
MYSTERY, HISTORY & HEART

WELCOME HOME, WEARY SOUL!

"G-good job, all!" Wendell said from behind them.

Sal felt around in the vines until he found a doorknob.

Thea grabbed his wrist. "Are you sure it's safe?"

"No," Sal admitted.

"I-it could be a t-trap," Wendell confirmed.

"Wonderful," Mona said, pushing the door open with a slow steady *creeeeeak*. She disappeared inside.

Sal nodded to his siblings. "It's not like we have another choice. Come on." One by one, they stepped inside too.

10

The Sweet Ralphie Tegen

The door's bell jingled as the Problim children and Violet crowded into a small, dusty lobby. It smelled like old books, dust, and blown-out candles. Memories, maybe, if memories had a smell. Overfull bookshelves lined the wall, and threadbare couches surrounded an old rug.

And there, again, was King Cat. He pounced up onto the counter beside the telephone as if he'd been there many times. Or maybe like he wanted a room. The cat cocked his head at the Problims, as if asking a question.

"Go away," Sal whispered to the feline. But the cat pounced into his arms, purring.

"Whoa!" Sal stiffened.

"It's a cat, Sal," Mona pointed out. "You're fine."

He shook his head. "I don't trust cats. They remind me of you."

"Thank you," she said sincerely.

"It's too bad Sundae's not here," Thea said. "Maybe the cat could tell her where to find Jeremiah Juice. Nobody speaks cat better than Sundae." She scratched the creature's soft head gently, and it nuzzled into her hand, purring more loudly.

Wendell walked to the front desk and pressed what he thought was the call button to get someone's attention. They were all surprised when the overhead lights blinked.

Immediately, a girl who seemed to be around their age ran into the room. She wore a summer-green dress. Her jet-black hair fell in braids over her shoulders. She had brown skin and dark eyes that seemed to sparkle with either mischief or happiness. (Mischief, Sal hoped.) She propped her arms on the counter and beamed. (Alas, just happiness.)

"Welcome to The Sweet Ralphie Tegen!" She was, Sal observed, very excited to have guests. "My grandma, Valley Payne, is the owner of this fine establishment. I'm her marketing manager, and I am thrilled that you're here! I'm Porsha Payne. Everyone calls me Pez. And before you ask, yes, I'm hearing-impaired. But I can still hear. Just try to look directly at me when you speak. I'm an expert lip-reader. Hi!"

If Pez hadn't just pointed out the small hearing aid in her ear, Sal wouldn't have noticed it at all. He wouldn't have asked about it either. Hearing aids were cool. What was not cool was the evil feline in his arms. He could smell its disgusting, fishy breath.

"I apologize for this cat," Sal said. "He is not trustworthy."

Pez laughed. "I know the cat. He's a regular here. All animals are pure of heart."

Sal turned to Mona and whispered, "No cat is pure of heart. I'm not sure we should trust this Pez."

But Pez's smile brightened. "If you're with King Cat, I trust you. Because that means you came here on the library ship."

"Yes!" Sal said. "We're looking for—"

The back door jingled and the lights flashed. "Sorry I'm late!" A woman with long, braided gray hair burst into the room. The style of her hair and the dress she wore were so similar to the girl's—it reminded Sal of how he used to try to match Grandpa. That was how he'd started wearing tools, because

Grandpa had worn a tool belt.

"Grammy," Pez said excitedly, pointing. "We have *guests*."

"WOO!" Grammy Payne clapped and spun around. And then she went very still, staring at the ragged children and fuzzy dog in front of her desk.

"Ms. Payne," Sal began.

"Call me Grammy Payne," she interrupted. "Everyone on the island does."

"Fine," he said, gently dropping the cat onto the floor. "We're looking for someone named Jeremiah Juice."

Pez's eyebrows floated up behind her glasses. She looked at her grammy and nearly spoke, before the lady silenced her.

"What for?" Grammy Payne asked, a suspicious look on her face now. The way she squinted at the children, to get a better look at them, caused a zillion wonderful creases at the corners of her eyes, like the rays on a setting sun. Sal could see that she had kind eyes even though she doubted them. He needed to put her at ease, and quickly, so they could get on their way.

"I'm Sal Problim. This is my family. We came

here because we're on an important quest. Our grandpa said Jeremiah Juice could help us finish it. We know Jeremiah hasn't sung on the island in years but . . . she used to like this place."

"She still likes this place," Pez said. Grammy nudged her.

"Is she close, at least?" Thea asked. "We really need her help."

"No," Grammy said. "She hasn't been here in years."

The Problim children looked at each other, worried. Now what? Sal thought. If Jeremiah Juice was gone, the whole riddle fell apart. They'd have to explore every single island in one day and—

"Grammy," Pez spoke softly. "They're good. I can tell. They came with King Cat!"

Grammy Payne drummed her long fingers on the countertop. "Frank Problim was a good man. He was on a good mission. He . . ." She let out a breath and closed her eyes. Then she looked Sal in the eye. "He looked a lot like you."

Sal's heart bloomed like a springtime garden at these words. *He* looked like Grandpa Problim? What did that mean? Did he have the same sparkle in his eyes? The same crease in his forehead? The same look on his face, maybe—the look of a real scientist?

"And Frank Problim," Grammy continued, "was the first one who called me Jeremiah Juice."

11

Frank Prohlim's Key

"That's awesome!" Sal yelled. He glanced back at his siblings. They were bouncing in delight. (King Cat stretched, yawned, and curled up on one of the sofas for a nap.)

"W-we need your h-help to f-finish Grandpa's r-riddle," Wendell offered.

"And we're very short on time," Sal added. "So if you could just—"

"Wait," Grammy Payne said. She didn't speak loudly, but something about the look in her eyes— and the authority in her voice—made them all go instantly quiet. This, Sal theorized, was probably a skill all grandmothers possessed. "First, I need to make sure you are who you say you are."

Sal shook his head. "How will you do that? It's not like we have kid IDs."

Grammy smirked. "I have my ways."

A strange answer, Sal thought. And the slightest worry crawled into his brain: What if Grammy Payne couldn't be trusted?

Pez cleared her throat and suggested they move to the formal meeting area, which was actually just a scuffed-up table to the side of the room. Pez and her grammy sat at the head of the table, looking over their guests. Sal sat at the chair closest to the door, just in case he needed to help his siblings make a quick escape. King Cat jumped on Pez's shoulder and curled its tail gently around her neck, like a fuzzy orange scarf.

Grammy Payne, who was . . . or had been . . . Jeremiah Juice, rested her hands on the table and looked at them all suspiciously. "We'll come back to the Jeremiah Juice thing in a second. Let's start here: Frank Problim used to stay in my fine establishment. He had a room that was his and his alone. Room number . . ."

"Seven," the kids said in unison.

"Lucky guess," Violet said to Pez. "He had a thing for sevens. . . ."

Grammy Payne nodded. "Yes. AND!" She slapped her hand down on the table, making them all jump.

"Frank Problim gave me a promise and a warning. The promise was that someday his seven grandchildren would come to the hotel, looking for something he left behind to help them on a terrible and wonderful quest."

"And here we are," Sal said abruptly. He wasn't trying to be rude. Grammy and Pez were probably cool people. But the Problims had a mission to complete! And yet . . . curiosity got the best of him. "What was the warning?"

Grammy Payne locked her fingers together, and stared at him. "He said that imposters might also come, pretending to be the Problim children. Now, as I said, you remind me of him. You with the, uh, scissors on your arms. Same face shape, you have. But the rest of you . . ."

Sal spun around and looked—Frida was hiding behind an old TV, only her fox ears visible.

"Full disclosure," Thea said, resting her hand on Violet's shoulder. "This is our cousin, Violet, and her very brave dog, Biscuit. Frida's here with us too. She's just shy. Our other sister, Sundae, is guarding the boat—"

"No matter," Grammy said, and she smiled. "I don't have a key to the room anyway. Only the real seven have the way inside. Frank told me he would make sure they had it."

Thea asked frantically, "What key?"

The kids began to rummage through their packs and blurt out ideas simultaneously.

"Maybe it's the water in the vial!" Mona suggested.

"Was it the b-bird?" Wendell asked.

"Maybe you sing it open?" Violet offered. "Like you do with the animal clues!"

"Wait . . . ," Sal said. Because he remembered . . .

That very first day in the Swampy Woods. That day only a few weeks ago when the house went kaboom and they found the old lunch box. Inside had been the first bone-stick . . . and also a key. It had come with a note:

For Sal,
A wise man who sets the world to blooming.

Sal reached around his neck and held up the key for Grammy Payne to see. "I have it."

Grammy smiled. She looked down at Pez who smiled too.

"Please follow me," Pez said, pouncing up out of her seat and racing toward the staircase. "We have an elevator if you prefer it, but these stairs are dreamy, aren't they?"

They were lovely, Sal had to admit. The stairs spiraled like the ones at the mansion. A strange zing settled in his heart at the thought of home. He didn't like the feeling, so he cleared his throat and spoke as they climbed.

"Is there anything else you can tell us?" he asked. "How did you know Grandpa?"

"We met when we were teenagers," Grammy said. She climbed the stairs slowly, so the Problims matched her pace. Even though Sal wished she would move a little faster. "He came over to the island with his best friend, Stanley. And they brought other friends with them—a couple of girls they were smitten with. We all had a grand time. We ate ice cream and danced under the string lights in the pavilion," she smiled. "Your grandparents told me I should sing. That I should share my songs. They thought up a stage name, Jeremiah Juice, and we put together a concert. A whole crowd of people flocked toward me when I sang. And so did tons of birds," she laughed.

Grammy reached the top of the swirled stairs and paused at the first floor, waiting for the Problems to gather around her.

"Grammy is like a princess in a fairy tale," Pez said, resting her hand on the woman's arm. "She sings and animals come to listen! It's enchanting . . . until the skunks show up."

"Why did you stop?" Sal asked. "Did something happen?"

Grammy shifted uncomfortably. Pez crossed her arms over her chest. "Tell them the truth. Why not?"

"I stopped because somebody wrote something rotten about me in the paper. I was embarrassed so . . . I quit singing in public. Now I only sing for Pez."

"That's it?" Sal asked. Thea nudged him in the side.

Grammy shrugged. "It is what it is. Follow me now." She meandered down the long hallway with Sal and his crew tight on her heels. Sal felt that same funny, and painful, bolt in his heart when he saw Pez loop her arm through her grandmother's arm. Seeing the two of them together hurt somehow.

The love of a grandparent is a powerful thing, he thought. A force unlike anything in science. And he missed his grandpa Problim. He kept hoping he was out there somewhere. But . . . clearly, Grammy Payne (or should he call her Miss Juice?) hadn't heard from him in years either. That wasn't a good sign.

"I w-wish we could h-hear you s-sing," Wendell said.

"Oh, my voice is no good anymore," Grammy said, waving them off. "According to that critic, it wasn't good then."

"That was only one person," Pez said.

"She said it sounded like a ton of gravel scraping across an empty parking lot," Grammy said.

"But other people said so many wonderful things!" Pez told her. "Who cares anyway? It's easy to talk about people doing things. Harder to do them."

"Enough," Grammy said. "What matters is that those were some wonderful years for me. This island became like a refuge for Frank and Stanley and their sweethearts."

The Problims glanced at each other. *Stanley.* Stan O'Pinion was the Big Bad, Sal thought. But was he as bad as Desdemona? As Cheese Breath?

"That's my grandpa," Violet said, as if she could

read their minds. As if she was trying to remind them to be careful with their words. Stan O'Pinion mattered to her. She chewed her lip in concentration. "Which means he's your grandpa too."

Sal stopped cold. So did his siblings. They all exchanged a sad look. It was an obvious truth. But it still surprised Sal. He hadn't really considered it . . . they had another grandpa. One who potentially hated them, but still.

"Now listen here," Grammy said, turning to face them when they reached the room. "Frank was doing top secret work on some important mission in Room Number Seven. . . ." Her voice trailed off as a shiver rolled over her shoulders. "Let's just say there are strange islands past the Miserable Mist."

Sal and his siblings leaned forward, as if they were hearing the most marvelous story.

"Is the mist really miserable?" Mona asked, with hope in her eyes.

"Some say it's enchanted," Grammy told her. "Or haunted, perhaps. That mist has wrecked hundreds of ships over the years. Supposedly though, if you break through that mist and actually see the islands— they're a wondrous sight. Most people aren't brave enough to try." Her eyes flickered. "Except Frank, of course. He was a brave man. Good thing, because past the mist come the enchanted bogs and quicksand pits and strange animals—"

The Problims nodded eagerly. Mona was beaming, and Sal knew why. She'd always wanted a quicksand pit of her own.

"And there are good kinds of magic too, I hear." Grammy's voice trembled. "Thin places."

"Like, places you have to suck in your belly to fit through?" Violet asked. "What if my helmet doesn't fit?"

"It's not like that," Grammy said, a smile tugging at the corners of her mouth. "A thin place is a little pocket in our world that feels so beautiful, so special . . . you can see or feel a glimpse of the world beyond this one when you come upon it. So I hear, anyway." She waved away the notion. "There's no time to think about it now."

Maybe not. But Sal felt tingly all over when Grammy mentioned a thin place. It sounded scientifically interesting, for one. It also sounded a little bit magical. Of course, they might not even exist at all. And it's not like he had time to find one if it did. Grammy was right: there was no time for daydreaming.

"Most people can't get through the Miserable Mist anyway," Grammy said. "Far too dangerous. And speaking of dangers." She waved toward the door. "Be very, very cautious in this room."

"Why?" Sal asked.

Pez and her grammy exchanged a knowing look. An odd look.

"There are things in this room in cages," Grammy said. "And they should stay in cages." With a sharp look at Pez, she continued, "You can show them inside. I have things to do downstairs."

Pez nodded firmly as her Grammy walked away. Then she turned to the Problems and said, softly, "There's a reason that we keep the door to Room Number Seven locked."

When the Squirrel
Met the Villain

There were actually four stowaways on Desdemona O'Pinion's tiny yacht. The first three were human, and they were presently terrified. LeeLee Alapo, Alabama Timberwhiff, and Noah Wong were hunkered down in the kitchen belowdecks. Bags of chips and donuts were crinkled and open all around them. And they were staring up into the face of an old man who looked very angry.

Or maybe just very confused.

"Hello," Stanley O'Pinion finally said.

The children were startled. LeeLee spoke up: "Hi."

Stanley began to speak, but LeeLee interrupted:

"If you plan to throw us off this boat, fine. We'll swim to find the Problems if we have to. They are our friends. And we won't let anybody hurt them."

Stanley had something important to say now. He felt the words rising in his chest before he spoke them, like a big billow of a wave about to crash on the beach. "I won't let anyone hurt them either," he admitted.

There. The words were out. So strange, he thought, how years and years of hate seemed to fall away as he spoke.

"I'll help you help them," he assured the stowaways. They didn't look afraid now, just confused. Stanley reached into the cabinet overhead for a package of Oreos. "Just be quiet down here," he said, "so my daughter doesn't hear you."

The boys looked at LeeLee, waiting for her approval. She crossed her arms, regarding Stan with narrowed eyes. "I thought you were the enemy. The Big Bad."

He felt a pang in his heart as he answered, "Who told you that?"

"Thea Problim. She said you had a feud with her grandpa years ago."

Stanley nodded, clutching the bag of Oreos over

his heart like a sugar shield. "That's true." He cleared the sadness rising in his throat. Sadness because there wasn't anger there now. There had been, all those years ago. Stanley thought Frank Problim could help him save someone he loved. His wife. His better-than-best friend. That magical water; only Frank knew where it was. What if a drop of it could have saved her? Frank refused to try. The water is evil, he'd told him. Stanley could remember the tears in Frank's eyes. "I would if I could," he said. "But it's not what you think. It's enchanted water. Evil water."

Stanley crouched down beside them and took an Oreo, offering it to Leelee. She didn't budge.

"I am not the Big Bad," he assured her. "Years ago, Grandpa Problim—Frank—was my best friend. We had a horrible misunderstanding. I was hurt over that. And then I lost someone I loved, and that kind of sadness . . . it can make you very angry at the world."

"Worse than angry," LeeLee said softly. "Grief's terrible. It'll turn you inside out."

Alabama nodded. "Loss is the worst. I understand." He nodded sympathetically at Stanley.

So did Noah. "I get it too. Grief is a monster, ya know?"

"I know," Stan said.

"I can't take back the years I lost," Stanley said. "But I believe, now, that Frank never meant to hurt me. He did the right thing. And sometimes the right thing feels like the most terrible thing. I want to help now. If I can."

"You certainly can," LeeLee said. "It's about time you did." She reached for the cookie.

"I'm assuming you have a plan, Miss . . ."

"Alapo," LeeLee said, reaching out her other hand to shake. "DeLisa Alapo. I go by LeeLee."

"I'm Stanley O'Pinion," he said, engulfing her hand with his. "I go by Stan." He nodded to Alabama. "I do like your suit."

The sequins on Alabama's pants seemed to sparkle when he smiled. "Thank you, sir."

"No time for compliments," LeeLee said. "Yes, we've been thinking of plans with Carly-Rue and Will. We could slow down the boat, maybe. Or sabotage any attempt to get the Problims. Carly-Rue is brainstorming up above."

"Good thoughts," Stan agreed. He turned his ear toward the slight commotion he heard nearby. "I might know someone else who can help as well."

He stood with a groan and whispered to the

children: "Stay put. And stay quiet."

"You're a fine man, Mr. Stan," LeeLee said, saluting him as he meandered through the belowdecks of the yacht, toward the small room he used as a study. He'd been hearing something down here for a while now. And . . . he'd seen something, he thought. Back when they boarded the yacht. He'd seen a flash of silver and purple. He'd forgotten about Frank's little robots until that moment. Frank's funny creatures had become Frank's little friends. Surely they no longer worked.

Stanley stepped into the study and propped his hands on his hips. "Snookums," he said softly. "Are you in here?"

A small *click-click-click* from behind him, and Stan turned to see Snookums the Squirrel perched on the edge of a desk. The squirrel's purple tail was trembling. Its small, silver hands were drawn up to its chest. And it stared at Stanley with sad gadget eyes that whirred. *How can a robot look sad?* he wondered.

"I won't hurt you," Stan said, moving slowly toward the squirrel. The squirrel did not look convinced.

Stan sat down in the squeaky swivel chair and

rolled close to the small creature. Creature, for that's what it was. It wasn't just a robot. Frank had made everything in his world come alive. Including Stanley's heart, once upon a time.

"You and I had a mutual friend once," Stanley said to the squirrel.

The squirrel flicked its tail and chattered in response.

"And my guess," Stanley said softly, "is that you are trying to help him, even now. You're trying to take care of his grandchildren."

The squirrel nodded, tapping its feet excitedly.

"Did you know," Stanley began, his voice thick with emotion, "they are my grandchildren too?"

The squirrel let out a sad chirp.

Stanley removed his glasses and bowed his head. Suddenly all the anger in his heart felt as though it were being poured out of a pitcher. And it made him feel . . . hollow. How much room had hate taken up inside him? For all these years, he could have been making memories with his grandchildren. He could have been a better grandfather, even, to Carly-Rue and Will. So much time had been wasted, all because of a grudge. All hate had ever done for him was make him feel very old. And very alone.

Something small and cold touched the top of his hand. He looked down to see a silver, robotic paw. Gadget eyes whirred, blinking up at him. How could a robot feel empathy?

Had love—Frank's love—made this creature come alive?

And if so, if that were true, there was no question about it: love was the most magical thing in the world. It was the only magic that mattered, really.

"Let's get to work," Stanley said. "Let's help Frank finish the job."

The squirrel bounced around happily on the desk, chattering and tapping its feet. The old man smiled, watching the squirrel celebrate.

Squirrels know a villain when they see one.

But squirrels also know that sometimes even the worst villains just need a friend.

13

Room Number Seven
at the Sweet Ralphie Tegen

Sal fitted his key into the lock, and Thea pushed open the door. A cloud of dust billowed out into the hallway, making every child except Violet cough. (Filtered through Violet's helmet, the room smelled like fresh-cut oranges.)

"Sorry," Pez said. "We clean all the rooms regularly. But this room is . . . moody. It's like it has a mind of its own."

"We like d-dust!" Wendell said. "This is f-fine." Then he sneezed so loudly he bounced backward.

"This is . . . a lab," Thea said, stepping inside. "Or . . . something."

Frida cartwheeled into the room. (And Sal

noticed, strangely, that neither Pez nor her grand-mother had looked at her even once.)

"A lab indeed," Frida shouted.

"A lab for me.
What are the wonders
the fox might see?"

Some of the wonders were typical of a hotel. There was a bed, nicely made, and a small table with a lamp. An old TV sat on the stand in the corner. But nothing about the rest of the room looked like a standard hotel room. The rest of the wonders were all Problim-approved: microscopes and files and boxes that surely contained all kinds of treasures. Or secrets.

"Maybe there are bones in the boxes," Mona said with a purr.

"We tried not to change it much," Pez said. "We've been hoping to see you for a long time."

"Why do you make this place so hard to find, then?" Thea asked.

Pez sighed. "We don't try to. I can't keep the ivy from growing. It covers up the windows and the doors every morning. So I tried to just . . . capitalize on it. Make it a cool factor. Know what I mean?"

Sal wasn't focused on Pez's marketing ideas. He was more enamored with the scene in front of him. A long table was set up in the center of the room, topped with a microscope, a basket of files, and a projector.

"And Bloomfizz!" Violet shouted, hoisting the six-pack above her head. "It's the special drink that makes you fly. Really fly!"

Mona's smile at this discovery reminded Sal of the Cheshire cat in *Alice's Adventures in Wonderland*.

"Definitely don't drink that," Thea said. "If it's been sitting there this long, it probably shoots you to the moon or something."

A shower curtain had been fitted to the ceiling, draping down to serve as a screen for the projector. It was a very efficient work space, Sal decided. He flung the curtain back with a *whish* to see what was behind it.

"Whoa . . . ," he said softly. Everyone went still, and stared at what was hidden against the wall: plants.

In cages.

The cages were propped in a row along the back

wall of the room. There were four of them, ranging in size from Tall-As-Thea to Tiny-As-Toot. The cages shouldn't surprise him, since Grammy had mentioned the room had caged things. But caged *plants*? He was happy to see that the plants were all bright green and taken care of. They bloomed out of old crates. Each plant had at least three thick stems full of leafy fronds. The thick stems narrowed to a large, speckled bloom that reminded Sal, at first, of a Venus flytrap. And then, the longer he looked, it reminded him of an alligator's head.

"You don't have to be afraid of these," Sal said, moving toward them. "I'm going to let them out and see what they—"

"No!" Pez was suddenly in front of him, holding her arms wide as if she was strong enough to keep him away. "I would advise against that. Strongly."

"Why?" Violet asked.

"We didn't cage the plants," she said. "Grammy said Frank Problim trapped these years ago." She whispered next, as if the plants were listening. (Which they probably were, Sal reasoned.) "They've never been watered."

"That's not possible," Sal said flatly. "They're so green."

Pez nodded slowly. "Riiight? And that's not all. If you get close to them . . . these are not nice plants. That's all I'm saying."

"Plants can't hurt you," Sal said.

"Unless they're poisonous," Mona clarified. "Or covered in spiders or something fabulous like that."

"Or unless it's Mona's flytrap," Thea offered. "It's thoroughly evil."

"Let's take a vote!" Mona shouted. "Who wants to open the cages and see what happens?"

"NO," they said in unison. Mona bowed her head in sorrow.

Pez glanced over her shoulder, staring at the plants like they were caged werewolves. This almost made Sal laugh. People were always so afraid of things they didn't understand. No matter though. He was an expert on plants.

Proof: these were Cave Bulbs. Totally common to underground water sources and *nothing* to be afraid of. They—like Wrangling Ivy—were harmless. But how were they so *green*?

"Trust me, Sal," Pez pleaded. "Leave them alone. But take a look around at everything else. And let us know if you need anything at all. We have room service, so call when you're ready for dinner."

Pez slipped out the door, leaving it open a crack.

Thea pushed aside the curtain in the window. Sal squinted at the sudden burst of light. Motes of dust sparkled through the air as he staggered to the window. From here, he could see the Library Ship docked in the harbor and the now-bustling streets down below.

"This is a good lookout spot," he nodded. "Let's get to work. See what we find here. Frida?"

The fox was suddenly beside him, looking up eagerly into his eyes.

"Will you go tell Sundae that we found The Sweet Ralphie Tegen . . . but it might take a while? And to alert us if anything happens?"

The fox puffed her chest in pride.

"Oh Sal,
this rocks!
The fox shall go
carry a message
to and fro.
And then, returning,
. . . not to boast . . .
that rotten lady
will not get close!"

"Excellent," Sal said. "I knew I could count on you."

Frida scampered out the cracked door and down the stairs—never making a sound.

Violet was watching Sal closely. He could have sworn she had a question in her eyes. But she shook her head and looked back at a pile of papers on the table in front of them.

"I will study those plans," Sal said quietly. "But first, let's find what we're after. Take anything you find about the cave. And look closely, because somewhere around here is the key to the Miserable Mist."

"Easy," Mona said. "We'll have what we need in an hour."

But the hour passed too quickly. Monday morning faded to lunchtime, then twilight, and then suddenly the Paynes showed up in the room with dinner. The sun was setting, but the Problims and Violet were still rummaging through Grandpa's makeshift office. They found everything from stale candy (weird) to a book about cave lakes in Mexico (awesome) to puppets (weirdly awesome).

"Boxes of slides," Sal shouted from the closet. He hoisted them above his head like a trophy as he emerged.

"W-what's a s-slide?" Wendell asked.

"That's one way people used to save pictures to show off in a big format," Sal told him. "I'll put this little slide into the projector here, and it will show up huge . . . probably on that shower curtain. It's way easier now with computers. But I think this is much more fun. Maybe there's something about the mist in here. . . ."

Sal opened a small box labeled "REALLY BAD PLANTS." He pulled the curtain back across the room, blocking his view of the Cave Bulbs. Then he grabbed some of the small slides from the box and pushed them into position in the back of the projector. With a faint *click*, the first black-and-white image appeared on the shower curtain:

Grandpa, young, standing in front of a boat with his hands in his pockets.

The Problim children all gasped.

"He does look like you, Sal," Violet observed.

Click!

Next slide: an island far off in the distance. It was hard to tell much about it in black and white.

"Is that the place where stars fall into the sea?" Thea asked. "It doesn't look starry."

Click!

Next slide: a jungle scene.

Click!

Then the mouth of a cave.

Click!

The next picture showed a lake, presumably in the cave since the image was so dark. It had been labeled "The Lake of Dreams/The Hub," and by the looks of Frank's smile, wasn't all together dangerous.

Click!

The next slide showed another cave. And this one looked . . . familiar.

"The clue," Sal said, fishing through his pockets to find the clue from Grandpa. "Do you remember that it mentioned a rabbit-shaped cave? Listen to this:

TOGETHER IS THE WAY TO REACH THE RIGHT END
WHERE A RABBIT-SHAPED CAVE CALLS YOU TO DESCEND. . . .

"I s-see b-bunny ears," Wendell agreed, pointing to the slide. Rocky spires were piled on top of the cave, casting a rabbitlike shadow.

Click!

Sal brought up the next slide.

A body of water . . .

"The f-fountain," Wendell breathed. "I know that's it. My f-fingers are t-tingling."

"Just from the picture?" Sal asked.

If this was the fountain of youth, it looked so simple. Like a swimming hole, really. Tall, leafy plants surrounded the pool.

"Cave Bulbs," Sal said softly.

He could see the shadows of the caged Cave Bulbs behind the shower curtain. They moved, barely, rustling as if a light breeze had blown past them.

But there was no breeze.

"D-did y-you see th-that?" Wendell asked.

"Probably just the air conditioner coming on," Sal said. He tried to ignore the way the tiny hairs on the back of his neck were rising.

"Are you sure that's the fountain?" Thea asked, pointing to the slide. It was like an oasis below the earth. It didn't look evil. And Sal wondered again if it even was.

As if she could read his mind (a scary thought), Mona cleared her throat and asked: "What if . . . it's not all bad?"

Thea nodded. "I've thought about that. I mean, Cheese Breath takes so much of it. What if a small amount is okay, even if a big gulp of it isn't?"

"Cheese Breath is proof," Sal reminded them. "He drank from the fountain. And now he's this jolty old bag of bones who would kill anybody to get more of it. It made him evil."

"Or he was already evil," Mona said.

"E-exactly," Wendell agreed.

Sal had no answer. And he wasn't sure how to get one.

"I'm curious," Violet said, "about why Frank didn't just destroy it back then."

"He c-couldn't," Wendell said. "N-not without d-dynamite. He didn't have the s-seven anymore."

"Why?" Mona asked.

"They'd all moved away from each other by then," Thea said, holding up files she'd been reading. "He saved newspaper clips about his siblings. One of them died in a war," she said sadly. "Others moved away, started families of their own. They didn't stay in the same place forever."

A sad quiet stretched between them. Why hadn't they stayed close? They were magical siblings, so surely they wanted to be together.

"Do you think . . . ," Mona asked, softly, ". . . they ever wished they'd drunk from the fountain? When they were older?"

Click!

Sal moved to the next slide. More plants—larger, fuller, twisted over the ground.

Click . . . and Sal blinked to make sure he wasn't imagining things.

The plant in the slide had a row of fine, razor-sharp teeth across its wide, flat leaves.

"I have a question . . . ," Violet said softly. Sal turned to see her looking at the tall plant. "Do you see . . . what I see? Down in the corner of the cage? There's something tangled inside the plant. It's almost like the plant is hiding it. I mean, I know plants can't do that, but . . ."

Sal pulled a telescope from his sleeve and ran beside her. In the far corner of the cage, in the midst of all the leafy green, Sal could make out a small shape of something spherical. Something like a globe. It looked about the size of a soccer ball, with the usual oceans and worlds painted across it. But there were words on it too, written sloppily by a marker.

"M-I-S-F. . . ," Sal read the letters he could see.

"Yes! That's got to be the key to the Miserable Mist. How did it get in there? No matter. Hold my spyglass, please."

"Why?" Violet asked. "What are you doing?"

"Isn't it obvious?" he said. "I'm opening the cage."

14

Really Bad Plants

Sal pulled a small pair of scissors from his sleeve and reached through the bars of the cage. He would trim the plant a little bit first, to see what it was hiding. His fingers were barely past the metal when the plant hissed—hissed!—and the large bulbs on top fanned open revealing rows of sharp, tiny teeth. Before Sal could move, the big plant twisted toward him like a snake, hissed again, and clamped down on his hand.

Sal screamed. He jumped up, feet landing on the side of the cage. He tried to pull his body—his hand—away before this plant ate him. What kind of Cave Bulb was this?!

Wendell's arms locked around his waist, yanking him back. But the plant gripped him tighter. Then Violet was beside him, grabbing the tiny axe that Sal kept affixed to his sleeve.

"STOP!" she shouted at the plant, her voice steely with authority. She hacked at the bars—trying to scare the plant—which worked. It spit out Sal's hand and ruffled its leaves.

Violet and Sal hit the floor with a hard thump. Sal's hand—all of it, thankfully—was still attached to his wrist. But an arched, bloody bite mark fell over his palm like a sinister rainbow.

"Can I take this plant home with me?" Mona asked hopefully, clasping her hands underneath her chin.

"I'll go get a first aid kit from Pez," Violet shouted, running out of the room. Biscuit bounded behind her, yipping.

Thea pulled a handkerchief from her pocket, kneeled down, and pressed it against the bite. "So much for that experiment."

"It might become infected," Mona reasoned, looking down at him. A lovely smile stretched slowly across her face. "What if the plant's fangs are poisonous? And your hand swells to ten times its normal size?"

Sal stood up, trembling. He barely had time to see Wendell's eyes grow very wide behind his glasses when a thick, writhing vine snagged around Sal's waist and pulled him back toward the cage.

A loud *chop* and Sal was free. A toothy leaf writhed on the floor before going still. This time they all ran to the far side of the room. Mona, Sal's axe in hand, stood a few feet in front of the cage as if she was daring it to move again. "This would make a fun pet," she said softly. Underneath her arm, she held a globe, which *she* had retrieved from the man-eating plant.

"What does the globe say?" Sal asked, standing up again.

Mona shook her head. "The globe does not speak, Sal. It's an inanimate object."

"What's written on it?" Sal asked, voice rising.

She held it out for him to inspect. "Nothing."

"But . . . ," Sal's voice trailed off in disbelief as he grabbed the globe, twisting it in his hands. "I saw letters!"

Pez, Violet, and Biscuit ran into the room then, first aid kit in tow. "Everything okay?" Pez asked.

"Fine," Sal said, his hand shaking as he held out the globe. "It tried to hide this from us."

Pez shook her head. "That's not ours."

Sal glanced back at the Cave Bulb. Plants were living things with their own personalities, but he'd never met one that had tried to hurt him. (Though he'd always assumed Fiona was plotting to do so.)

"We tried to warn you," Pez said.

"It's fine," Mona said. And she glared at Sal and grinned. "I saved him. As usual."

This was officially the second *worst* day of his life. The first was losing Toot. But this situation was also horrific: Mona had rescued him. Ugh. He would never live this down. Ever.

"Amazing!" Pez said. "They've never been watered. But they still have a fighting spirit."

"The fountain water," Thea said softly—just to Sal. "It kept the plants alive all these years. But it made them something different. Something violent."

"Proof," Sal said. "Like Cheese Breath is proof! The water *can* make you live longer, but it changes you." He glanced down at the bite mark on his hand. "Would living be worth it if you became some monstrous version of yourself? Something vile and vicious and mean?"

"It could be fun," Mona said. They all glared at her.

"Well, it could!" she countered.

"I-if that's t-true, Cheese B-Breath gets m-more h-horrible anytime he drinks f-from it," Wendell said.

"I think so," Sal agreed.

Violet spoke up. "I don't care for Auntie Desdemona. But . . . I really don't think she knows how bad the water is. I think she wants to bottle it, sell it, maybe. She's thinking she could make millions selling it as a serum. Something to keep people from aging. Surely she doesn't know what it really does. If she did, this whole feud—this whole history—would be over. Grandpa Stan must not have believed it either. If he could see this, if he knew . . ."

Sal knew that Frank had tried to tell Stanley O'Pinion that the water was vile. But Stanley hadn't believed Grandpa Problm. He'd wanted the water to save someone he loved. He must have felt like love was stronger than science, Sal thought. Was it? Ever?

"Hold on," Thea said, her eyes shining with an idea. "Sal thinks he saw letters on the globe, right?"

"I don't *think* I did," Sal clarified. "I know I did."

"Then the globe is keeping a secret," Thea said,

smiling. "Mona! Where's the drop of water you found in the Pirates' Caverns?"

Mona took the cap off the vial and passed it to Thea. "What if that's fountain water?"

"It's n-not," Wendell assured them. "I can t-tell."

"It says it reveals secrets," Thea said.

Mona grabbed her wrist. "Don't use all of it then. Imagine what we could do with that."

Sal trembled at the thought.

Thea poured it onto the globe and words illuminated.

"L-like s-secret ink!" Wendell shouted.

Faint at first, then starker, more brightly, the words appeared:

MISERABLE MIST SURVIVAL MANDATE
1. TELL THE MIST WHAT YOU ARE CALLED.
2. TELL THE MIST WHO YOU ARE.
(JEREMIAH WILL KNOW THE DIFFERENCE.)

"Where is she?" Sal asked Pez. "Where's Grammy Payne? We have to get going!"

"She went to the beach," Pez said, as Sal ran out of the room.

"Everyone pack up while I'm gone," Sal yelled over his shoulder.

"Be careful out there," Violet said. "There's a storm coming."

"There's worse coming than a storm," Thea said, her voice fading as Sal ran down the stairs. "I can feel it in my heart."

The Scientist

Sal ran down the now-quiet streets of the Isle of St. Maria with the globe in his non-bitten hand. The windows in town were filled with warm yellow light. He saw families huddled inside, eating slowly and talking. He saw old couples and young couples and one lady who was sharing a bowl of spaghetti with her little dog. It was such an odd feeling to realize there was a story happening in every window that he was no part of whatsoever. That there were so many places in the world, with so many people, that he'd never seen.

Thunder rumbled gently overhead. Why had Grammy gone to the beach when a storm was coming? He'd become suspicious of everyone now, thanks to Ari. Miserable Ari.

Ari who had his baby brother.

Ari . . . who *had been* his friend. She'd done a really good job deceiving him. She'd faked him out. And it was painful and also embarrassing. So how could they be 100 percent sure this old woman—this Jeremiah Juice—was their friend too?

When Sal finally reached the boardwalk out to the sand, he saw two people:

First, he saw Grammy, strumming a guitar by the water's edge.

Second, he saw Frida the Fox, sitting a ways behind her in the sand, pretzel-style, swaying to the music. Sal had to blink at the sight of his sister. For one strange second, Frida seemed to . . . glow. If anybody walked by and glanced at her, they might think there was a tiny bonfire on the beach. Not a little girl wearing a fox-eared hoodie. Another hard blink, and she was perfectly clear again. Just an orange fox. Not a beam of light.

He settled into the sand beside her, panting from his quick walk to the beach. Grammy looked very happy right now. It would be rude to interrupt. He'd give her seven minutes until he asked for help. But only seven. They had to get on their way. The rain began to fall, cool and gentle, making freckle-dots all around them.

Sal was mesmerized by Grammy Payne's music. She strummed her guitar, playing for no one besides the fox and the sea. A pink bird floated down from the sky and perched on the neck of the guitar. Then came a blue bird, and another the color of a bright dandelion. It was as if they were all gathering in anticipation, hoping she would sing. Frida spoke softly:

"When I gaze upon the sea
I think of the rhyme that's just for me."

Sal nodded. "I think about that too. Everybody else's ability makes sense already. Wendell is water. Toot is air. I'm earth. You're—"

"Fire," Frida said, and her eyes seemed to spark at the words.

"My love for family makes me shine," she
    reminded him.
"That's how the power becomes mine.
I love and love and try to let go. . . ."

Frida squished her eyes shut and wiggled her fingers toward the sea. Sal watched . . . but nothing happened.

"But what happens next?" Frida asked, and shrugged.

"I still don't know."

He didn't either. Fire. Could she create fire out of anything? Start a fire with her mind? Thank goodness that wasn't Mona's power, he decided.

"I'll help you figure it out," he promised her. "Don't forget what Grandpa said. Some gifts take time to discover. But the wait makes it even more special."

Frida smiled. She pushed the sand together, making a tiny castle. A little kingdom of her very own.

"You okay, kid?" Grammy Payne was suddenly standing in front of him, guitar held against her side. He hadn't even noticed the music stopping. Frida the Fox—ever sneaky—had already disappeared. How did the fox move so quickly, he wondered.

"I wasn't trying to spy on you," Sal said. He held up the world in his hands. "We found the way through the mist. But I don't understand it."

"I see," she said, and she cocked her head at the

expression on his face. The storm was close, dancing all across the nearby sky.

She reached for the globe in Sal's hands and read the instructions.

"Your grandpa and his riddles," she said. The smile that reached across her face was a sad one. "This is what he used to tell me, when a critic hurt my feelings. Something like it, at least. It doesn't matter what you are called. What matters is who you are. . . ."

Sal groaned. That sounded like some mantra from a Midge Lodestar show. "That doesn't make any sense to me."

Grammy shook her head and sat down beside Sal in the sand. "What you are called—your name—is just a name. You can change your name, if you want. That's what I did when I sang." She shrugged. "And I did it because I thought maybe it wouldn't hurt if someone made fun of me. If they didn't like my voice, I mean."

Lightning crackled the faraway sky. "But," she added, "whenever you are living a true adventure—living a good life—someone will tease you for it. And then you have to remember who you are. You, for example, are resilient. You are a scientist. You are a good brother and a good friend; I can see that."

Sal almost laughed. "I let my little brother get kidnapped. I'm a horrible brother."

Grammy grinned. "A bad babysitter, perhaps. But a fine brother. Walk me back to the hotel."

Grammy moved fast; she knew Sal was on a deadline. He was grateful for that.

"The bravest sailors in the world have turned around in the middle of that mist. Because it does things to you . . . makes people see things. From what I hear." She shrugged. "I was never brave enough to try. I wasn't even brave enough to sing again after one bad review. So I'm definitely not floating through haunted fog."

"Haunted?" Sal asked.

"Some people see ghosts," Grammy said, turning down the street toward the inn. "Or monsters. You might see your nightmares come to life. The Miserable Mist becomes whatever you are most afraid of. It is where fear lives, in its most raw and terrible form. Apparently, this," she tapped the globe, "is how your grandfather got through. Interesting. I just assumed he used a fog lamp."

"So I just shout that I'm Sal Problim? That's it? And the mist doesn't bother me?"

Grammy groaned. "What did I just say? The mist doesn't care what you're called," she clarified. "The mist will yield to who you are." She poked his chest with her gnarled finger. "In here. At least you'll have a whole crew to help you get through it. Frank went through it alone. It'd be a terrible thing to tackle alone."

Sal would prefer doing it alone, actually. Sometimes his siblings got on his nerves, Mona especially. But he didn't want to see any of them in real pain. Not for a second.

"I'm still lost on what to do exactly," Sal admitted.

"You'll figure it out."

"Have you?" Sal asked, opening the door for them both. The room smelled like fresh-baked pies.

"What do you mean?" Grammy asked, hanging her jacket on the hook by the door.

Sal pointed to her old guitar. "Years ago, you let some person—who is probably just jealous they don't have the skill or guts to make music of their own—keep you from singing ever again. You make music. That's the same as making magic!"

Grammy bit her lip and looked down at the floral-patterned carpet of the hotel. Sal had never interacted much with any adults besides his parents.

But he was beginning to see adults needed just as much encouragement as he did. That they still had fears and worries. Which made sense, he guessed. Adults were just grown-up kids.

Sal heard a slight noise at the door, like squeaky boots coming to a fast stop—followed by a sharp banging. Pez ran downstairs. "Another guest!"

Sal felt a bolt of warning shoot through his chest. They'd been here too long. Desdemona was rotten, but she wasn't stupid. Sal's only comfort was that the hotel was only found by the pure of heart. But what if Desdemona just paid some kindhearted person to bring her here?

"Wait," Sal said, spinning so fast his tools clattered. "Don't open that—"

Pez had already pulled the hidden door open . . . and outside stood a flustered (but still crowned) Carly-Rue O'Pinion.

Before Sal could ask what she was doing there, she grabbed his shoulders.

"Y'all have to leave. Mom's on her way. She knows where you are. Run!"

16

The Great Escape
(and a Songbird's Return)

"Carly-Rue," Mona said, running down the stairs to greet her former nemesis. "How did you get here? Why aren't you celebrating your win?"

"Because I am rescuing you, Mona Problim." Carly-Rue said this proudly, adjusting her crown as she spoke. "Any true queen cares for her friends."

Sal fought the urge to barf. This was far too sentimental.

"You shouldn't have come here," Sal told her. "For one—we're quite good at getting ourselves out of terrible fiascos. For two—no offense—your mom is out of control and she'll follow you."

"She doesn't have to follow me!" Carly-Rue said.

"She knows about this place. That's why I—"

"And," Sal continued, "this mission is dangerous. We thrive on danger. But I don't recommend it for everyone."

"Oh, I do," Mona said. "Life would be so boring without danger. How would you ever know what you were made of if you didn't risk your life now and then?"

"Shush!" Carly-Rue held up her hands as if she was calming down a room of pageant contestants. "Enough! I'm trying to tell you that my mother—your enemy—is in this town right now, looking for you. So she'll be here in no time, if she isn't already. You need to skedaddle off this island immediately or—"

"She'll split us up," Thea said sadly from the top of the stairs. "Send us to seven different continents."

"And T-Toot needs u-us," Wendell said from beside his twin.

"And I'll never be able to come out of my room again," Violet added. Sal noticed that her face had paled considerably behind her mask. Violet looked like she was seasick on land. "Is my dad with her? Is he mad at me?" Biscuit brushed up against her leg comfortingly.

Carly-Rue nodded, sending stray blond curls bouncing around her head. "But we can talk some sense into him later."

Violet's lip trembled. "I don't know what's worse—the thought of not being able to leave my room ever again or the thought of Dad being mad at me."

"Als-so," Wendell said, "i-in case you a-all forgot, we actually d-did break into their h-house. I mean, she's g-got stuff on us now."

Sal nodded, processing this entire predicament quickly in his mind. His mind—the best computer. The ultimate Problim problem solver. "Don't worry. We've got what we need anyway. I know how to defeat the Miserable Mist. Once we get past that, there's got to be some island that looks starrier than the others. I hope. Pack up everything we need from upstairs and let's go!"

The siblings raced back to Room Number Seven with thundering steps. The Problims gathered their backpacks and any small pictures or doodles from Grandpa's workroom that looked important. Frida the Fox burst into the room in a gold-orange blur. Sal blinked, hard. Why did his sister look like she was glowing again?

"Basement!" Thea shouted, shuffling past him. "Frida says there's a way out from the basement!"

A puzzled expression pinched Carly-Rue's face.

The Problims scrambled down the hallway.

"I'm glad you dropped by," Mona said to Carly-Rue, as they all herded down the corridor. "Thank you for your help."

Now—even with the enemy almost at the door—Sal had to come to a full stop. "What?" he nearly shouted.

His siblings turned to look at him. "What," he clarified, "has happened to Mona?" He studied her suspiciously. "Are you faking being nice to get something you want?"

"I like Carly-Rue," Mona said. And then with a shrug, as if it was the most normal thing in the world she added: "People can change. People do change. Think about how much we've changed in the last two weeks."

"N-no t-time for philos-s-s-ophical th-thoughts," Wendell said, waving them forward. "Let's g-go."

"Wait," Sal shouted, as they reached the top of the stairs. "Listen." He readjusted the globe he was carrying. If Toot were with them, he'd fire off a warning fart right about now, because the front door was opening. The Problim children backed up, and crouched down on the ground of the second floor. Sal heard the loud click of high heels banging across the lobby floor. He breathed slowly, so his tools wouldn't make even the slightest noise.

"Can I help you?" Grammy Payne said.

WHAP! It sounded like someone had slammed their hand down on the counter.

Then came the unmistakable hiss of Desdemona O'Pinon's voice: "I know they're here. And if they don't come out, they'll be very sorry."

17

A Queen Leads the Way

"Oh no," Thea whispered. "We're doomed." The Problims stayed hunkered down in a huddle at the top of the spiral stairs, out of sight from the front desk. Sal leaned forward, slowly, to peek through the bars. He could barely see Desdemona O'Pinion's silhouette.

"W-we're too late," Wendell agreed.

"How will we get to the basement now?" Carly-Rue whispered.

Sal was busy thinking. Good news: Desdemona didn't have any authorities with her. Bad news: from what he could see, she had two accomplices. Sal couldn't make out the first. But the second was . . .

"I'm here for my daughter!" Joffkins shouted. "I don't care about anybody else. I just want my daughter!"

Sal felt Violet cringe beside him.

"Who is the other one?" Thea whispered.

"Stanley!" Grammy called out. "I barely recognized you! It's been so long!"

"Uh oh," Sal whispered, as a shiver of panic raced through his heart.

"Grandpa?" Violet whispered. "He actually left the house?"

"That's only three," Sal said. "But they'll grab us if we go through the front door. We have to get to the basement. But they'll see us if we run down the stairs! Help me think, Violet. Would Wrangling Ivy help?"

Violet shook her head quickly. "That could hurt Grandpa."

Mona sighed and said with relish, "I'll have to trap them downstairs somehow. Create a diversion so you all can run for it."

"No," Thea argued. "We have to stay together."

Stanley and Grammy were hugging, talking about old times, laughing like long-lost friends. Then Desdemona slammed her hands down on the front desk again, startling all the children. "I know they're here. Someone told me the boy with the swords came in here!"

Sal's shoulders tightened. "I don't have swords," he whispered. "They're gardening tools."

"Shhh," Thea cautioned. She nodded back toward the conversation happening down below.

"Valley here says she hasn't seen them," Stan said, resting his hand on Desdemona's shoulder. "Let's get back to the boat and regroup. I'm sure they—"

"I'll find them myself," Desdemona said, pushing away from him.

Grammy zoomed around the desk, blocking Desdemona's path. Or pausing it, at least. She was doing her best to give the Problem children time to run. Or hide. But Sal could see—there was no way to do either.

"We could cause an earthquake," Mona said.

Sal shook his head. "We'd smash the hotel."

"I could pounce on them,
defeat them.
I'll beat them all down!
Get ready,
stay steady,
the fox will come down."

Frida was suddenly beside Sal. She always moved so quickly.

"Careful Frida," Thea said to her little sister. "They'll see you."

Sal heard Carly-Rue whisper as she leaned into Violet: "What is she looking at, and who is she talking to? *Who is Frida?!*"

And then . . . the lights flashed behind them.

"It's Pez!" Violet whispered to everyone. Pez stood behind them at the end of the hallway, hands on her hips. "There's another way to the basement," she mouthed. And she motioned for them to follow. The Problims raced down the hallway, ducking into an empty bedroom just as Desdemona and Joffkins climbed the stairs. Sal heard Desdemona at the door. And then he heard the wild sound of a hiss.

"There is a cat in my hair!" Des shouted. "GET IT OUT!"

King Cat had been an ally after all, Sal realized. Maybe all cats weren't evil. Pez waved the Problims deeper into the room, and they followed, scampering so their feet wouldn't be heard along the old carpet. Then Pez shoved a nightstand away from the wall.

"I-is it a secret pass-sageway?" Wendell asked. "Or . . ."

"An old laundry chute," Sal clarified. "You first, Frida."

Carly-Rue and Violet shot each other a strange—and very surprised—look. Frida turned a cartwheel, and then jumped feetfirst into the chute.

Thea, Wendell, Mona, and Violet followed. Just as Sal was about to thank Carly-Rue for her help—so she could return to her mom—Carly-Rue pulled off her crown and held it tight to her chest, hitching up her leg to climb into the chute.

"What are you doing?" Sal asked, though he knew the answer already. And he knew he wouldn't like it one bit.

"I'm going with you," she said, as if this was the obvious solution. As if she was needed. And . . . maybe she was?

Sal remembered the clue that set them off on this adventure: *find an O'Pinion and do make amends. . . .*

He thought Grandpa had meant Violet. But Violet was only one and . . . did he want more O'Pinion kids involved in this somehow?

Desdemona would be even madder if Carly-Rue came. The search would be even more intense. And, if they failed, the punishment would be even more severe.

But . . . what if Carly-Rue had to be there too, to fix all this? He didn't protest as she disappeared down the chute.

And now he stood alone with Pez. "We'll come back," he said at the sad look on her face.

"I understand," she said. "I'll miss you guys."

"You're doing a marvelous job with the hotel," he told her.

"Thank you." She smiled. "We hope you enjoyed your stay."

Sal smiled. He had enjoyed it. Very much.

He jumped into the chute . . . not realizing how loudly the globe—plus the tools on his sleeves—would clang, boom, and ting all the way down.

18

The Stowaways

Sal thumped onto the concrete floor of the basement, which smelled like dust and laundry detergent—a #150.[6] His siblings grabbed him, silencing his sleeves.

"What was that noise?" Desdemona was yelling from up above them now. "Are you hiding them? They're thieves! Urchins! I'll search every room until I find them!"

"You've got to get rid of this jacket," Mona said.

---

6 **#150**: The Fine Young Scholar: Smells like dust and laundry detergent. Emitted when Toot is having a brilliant thought or observation.

"It's been slowing you down all along. But now it's actually a risk."

"Leave it alone," Sal said to her through clenched teeth. "My jacket is part of me. It's like my third arm. I can't take it off!"

Thea held a trembling finger over her mouth. *Shhhhh.*

"Come on," Carly-Rue whisper-yelled, grabbing Sal's hand. "There's the window!"

Sal grabbed a hand too—he wasn't sure whose—and they ran for the window in the corner of the basement. The cousins made a human ladder and hoisted one another up and outside. Sal's sleeves made it hard to get through the tiny opening, but he finally burst onto the cobblestone street of the Isle of St. Maria. They were in an alleyway beside The Sweet Ralphie Tegen, their shadows illuminated by a flickering streetlight. Night had pressed in close, and this was good. Night would help them leave.

Sal pulled a compass from his sleeve. He took seven seconds to map the escape in his mind. First, run down the alley. Then turn right at the corner and run past the hotel (quickly, so Desdemona wouldn't see them pass by if she happened to be back at the door by then). That road would take them back to the town square, and from there, the ship was easy to find.

"Come on," Mona whispered. It made sense that she would lead since it was so dark. He had to at least try to trust her.

They scrambled up the alleyway, toward the front of the building.

"A few more steps," the fox said, her breath heavy from excitement.

"Turn right past the door.
Then all is right
with all the world."

Suddenly, just as they reached the edge of the alley, Mona crouched down behind a pile of boxes stacked for recycling. She grabbed Sal's sleeve and pulled him down too. Then everybody ducked. Mona shook her head no, and pointed through the crack between the boxes.

"Rats," Sal whispered. About ten police officers huddled around the door of The Sweet Ralphie Tegen. That was a lot of people to run past without getting snatched.

"You should have let me keep one of the cage plants," Mona told them.

"That w-wouldn't have h-helped!" Wendell said.

Something soft brushed against Sal's hand, and he was startled. When he looked down to see King Cat staring up at him, he nearly screamed.

"King Cat helped facilitate our rescue," Thea reminded him.

King Cat licked his paws as if this was a perfectly normal evening.

"Maybe if the fox scares the policemen," Thea said, "we can run?"

Frida shook her head yes, ears flopping happily.

Carly-Rue shook her head. "What the heck is *the fox*?"

"Frida!" Sal whispered. He pointed to the fox, who sat right beside Carly-Rue.

"Shhhh," Thea whispered. Even in the dark, Sal could see her tremble. He glanced through the crack and watched the police officers. They were babbling into walkie-talkies. And they were way too close to the boxes where the Problim children were hiding.

Sal did a speedy brainstorm: they couldn't cause an earthquake. That could hurt someone, or mess up these beautiful buildings. They couldn't use Wrangling

Ivy—it would take too long. They couldn't call on the water, because that was dangerous too. They were really, truly stuck. Sal held his breath. Thea reached out for his hand. A circus spider crawled out of her sleeve, and up his arm, which made him shiver. But he was grateful to have her beside him.

What if he lost them all?

He wished he could make them invisible. Ask some big island plant to hide them, just like the Cave Bulbs had hidden the globe. They were his world after all. He wished he had some sort of magical power that would hide them from people—from any person, ever—who might try to hurt them. But he had nothing to help them right now. Just gardening tools. Which scraped the stone street as readjusted himself.

"Shhhh," Thea said softly. "*Stop* squirming, Sal."

Sal froze . . . which somehow dislodged the globe in his hands. It thumped against the cobblestones and rolled. Wendell slapped his hands down on it to make it stop.

A policeman jerked his head toward the boxes. He pulled his walkie-talkie from his belt. "They're in the recycling pile," he said. And waved his team

toward them. They were paces away.

"We're caught this time," Sal said softly. "I'm sorry. It's my fault." They all gripped each other tightly, waiting to be yanked out of the pile one by one.

And then a sharp shout came from down the street. "Hey! Police officers! We're the Problim children! Come get us!"

The officer spun toward them. "Is that kid wearing sequins?"

"My crew showed up!" Carly-Rue exclaimed in a whisper.

Sal leaned around the boxes to see Will O'Pinion, Alabama Timberwhiff, Noah Wong, and LeeLee Alapo standing on a picnic table at the end of the street—in the opposite direction of the town square—waving wildly. The cops turned, racing toward them.

"Let's go!" Mona said, pulling her brother's hand.

And then a sweet sound filled the air, from the doorway of The Sweet Ralphie Tegen. Everyone on the street went still. The Problim children listened as the most beautiful, gentle guitar music Sal had ever heard echoed down the street. The music was joined by a voice.

Sal knew, even then, he would never be able to describe the way the song sounded. But he would always remember how that song made him feel: like watching a sunset. Like the joy of seeing a root push through the dirt for the very first time. Grammy Payne's voice was low, just rusty enough to sound unique, rippling as it rose over octaves. Before the rainbow-canaries even floated down the alleyway toward the sound, the Problim children knew what was happening.

Grammy—aka: Jeremiah Juice—was performing again on the Isle of St. Maria.

Suddenly, families were running down the street—hand in hand—in disbelief. One elderly couple hobbled down the sidewalk, tears streaming down their faces, reaching for the music as if it was a thing they could touch. Crowds of people were leaving their houses, walking toward the hotel, laughing and smiling. Soft rain began to fall, as if the sky was so happy it decided to cry. People danced all along the shiny streets.

Every police officer was transfixed by the small

woman standing in front of the ivy wall. Her eyes were closed. Her long fingers scrambled over the guitar. Her voice tangled with the seaside melody.

"Come on!" LeeLee shouted. She was with the Problims now, along with Will, Noah, and Alabama. "She's giving us enough cover to get out of here!"

"Let's go, King Cat," Sal said, scooping the beast up into his arms. "I suppose I'll carry you." The creature purred as Sal ran. Wendell raced ahead of him, carrying the globe.

The Problims and their friends blended easily into the dancing mass and down the street.

And yet, just before the children turned the corner to run for the boat, Sal saw Carly-Rue pause. She turned back and whispered, "Sorry, Mom."

And Sal paused too. Even though he was in a hurry. He looked back because the hair on his neck prickled like someone was watching him. And someone was: Stanley O'Pinion. Sal knew he should run, but he couldn't look away.

"Which way did they go?" Desdemona was yelling from the doorway of the hotel, shoving the crowd out of her way. "Father, do you see them??"

Sal's eyebrows lifted. He waited for Stan O'Pinion

to point him out. He was looking right at him, Sal was sure of it.

"They ran back into the hotel, I think," Stanley said, and he turned away. He ushered his daughter back inside.

How . . . odd. Maybe he hadn't seen them after all. He couldn't have, could he?

No time to ponder. Sal ran along behind his siblings. Frida the Fox led the way through the night, shining—Sal observed—as brightly as a torch. There was no question in his mind now; Frida Problim was coming into her element. And it might be even more magical than he'd imagined.

19

The Tragic Tale
of Ari O'Leary

Tuesday morning was bright and cheery, a sharp
contrast to everything about the old ship belong-
ing to Augustus Snide—the man whom the children
called Cheese Breath. The ship was docked near
DuVerney Island. DuVerney, a tiny barrier island
farthest west from the mainland, was a hidden
haven for only the wealthiest clients. Ari knew this.
She'd anchored the ship in DuVerney before. And she
knew that every so often, amid the wild beauty of
this small island, terrible people sorted out their bad
business. She assumed this was true, at least. Why
else would the old man come here?

And why was he here today? He was meeting the

Problim children on Wednesday. That plan hadn't changed, had it? He'd promised he wouldn't actually hurt them.

From the small window in Ari's room, she could see a distant wall of mist, which, according to legend, hid the most magical islands from the fearful. And the evil. The old man would never admit it, but he'd always been too afraid to penetrate the fog. He was waiting for the Problims to do it first—to make sure it was safe. Then they'd lead him through and escort him to the fountain. Eventually. But he had other matters to attend to right now.

She checked the time, steadied herself, and picked up the baby from the floor where he'd been playing with a small teddy bear.

"His meeting's about to start," Ari explained. "I have to let him know." Toot held on to her shoulder,[7] and together they walked the creaky hallway to the farthest door.

Ari knocked loudly. She didn't rap or tap against it; she banged on the door. In small ways, she needed to make her presence known.

---

7 **#181:** The Explorer: Smells like a city street on garbage day. Used to signify that brave young Toot is ready to make new discoveries and see new places and possibly get his diaper changed.

"Come in here, girl," came the old man's throaty voice.

The room was dank and smelled like mold. The curtain was pulled over the window behind him, a slip of light pressing through the hem. Ari held the toddler extra tight. And Toot held her too. At first, she thought he was afraid when he held her like this. But no—she could feel it now. Toot was protecting her.

Augustus didn't look at her. He sat at his desk. His jacket hung loosely from his shoulder bones, bulky and threadbare. He was studying maps, like always. "What?" he barked.

"Sir," she said. "Your meeting is about to begin. Your guest is waiting for you at the villa. I made sure."

"Only one of them?" the man asked. And now he met her gaze head-on. When he didn't wear sunglasses, his blue eyes looked milky and marbled. It was an unsettling sight. "The old man isn't there?"

Funny, Ari thought, *Augustus Snide calling anybody else old.* "Just the lady," she informed him. "Should I go with you?"

Cheese Breath chuckled. "Of course not. You may stay on the boat and complete your chores and tend to *that*." He waved toward Toot.[8]

Since Ari had gone to live with Cheese Breath, that's all she'd done: chores. There were floors and toilets to clean. Decks to be swabbed and scrubbed. There were lightbulbs to replace and dinners and breakfasts and lunches to prepare. Once she did all that, Cheese Breath didn't care what else she did.

So she stayed in her room. Ari had a few belongings that she kept in a red backpack: an old camera; someone had given one to everyone at the kids' home. A ragged novel about a brave little mouse. A teddy bear, which was babyish, maybe. She'd let Toot cuddle the bear since he came aboard. For years, it had made her feel safe at night. That's the only thing she'd had with her at the children's home when she'd arrived there. The only hint that she'd ever been wanted.

Cheese Breath pushed up from his desk and rounded the table, his hat low over his face. Toot hissed as the man walked by.

"Careful, little baby," Cheese Breath said to the child. "What if your siblings don't come for you?

---

8 **#45**: The Braveheart Fart: The toot used by Toot to summon his courage and drive fear into his enemies' hearts. Smells like moldy cheese and sweaty victory.

What if they decide they're fine the way they are? I can make your life miserable."

Toot made a noise that could only be described as a growl. Not a fearsome one; it was more like a little dog's growl. Then he made a noise that was definitely a toot.[9]

"It's okay," Ari said, comforting the baby. And herself too.

Even though Ari knew the old man was telling the truth.

Cheese Breath staggered down the hall. Arianna settled Toot back on the floor of her room. "Want to follow me while I do chores? Or do you want me to make a place for you to nap?"

Toot tooted.[10] Then he looked directly into Arianna's eyes. For the first time, he looked like he was about to cry. She hoped he didn't. Because that would make her cry, she knew. She crouched back down to eye level again. And he pressed his tiny hand against her cheek.

---

9 #1: The I-Want-My-Mommy Fart: Smells like spoiled milk and mashed bananas. Toot's most desperate plea in times of deepest distress.

10 #27: The Once-upon-a-Toot: A fart that occurs when Toot Problim wants to hear a story, or have a book read to him. Smells like musty old books, and one's own armpits after a weeklong hike in the heat.

It was such an affectionate gesture that it took her by surprise. *He feels sorry for me*, she realized. He *is the kidnapped one, and he's feeling sorry . . . for* me?

"Cheese Breath says your family is born with a strange, wild magic," Ari said, reaching to touch Toot's face the same way he was touching hers. She wondered if something might happen. But no.

"Do you want to know where I came from?" Ari asked.

Toot's eyes widened. He nodded. She picked him back up and carried him into her room, stopping in front of the window. Rain made silver scars across the glass.

"I only ever remember being in the group home. And it wasn't like in the books, ya know. No orphans scrubbing the floors or anything. It was okay. There were lots of us. The caretakers were kind. Of course, you always hope you'll find a family. And one girl— a good friend of mine—got adopted. She lived with a fun lady who gave her a room she got to paint. She has a dog now and plays guitar and goes to a great school. She feels . . . loved. I guess it's awful corny to say, but I'd like to be loved by something. By a pet. And by a person."

Toot tooted again.[11] *He was like his own little symphony*, Ari thought. (A really stinky one, but still.) The stink was as rank as all the rest of them, and she wrinkled her nose. Ari knew this was actually Toot's way of trying to talk to her. Maybe he wanted to know more. Maybe he just wanted her to talk.

"So one day, I found out I had been adopted. Or had a new caretaker at least. Where I'm from, that's what they call someone who takes care of a kid who has nobody to look after them. I was so happy. The lady who came to pick me up was as lovely as you'd imagine anybody to be. Professional, you know? Really pretty smile. I thought—*Wow, this is it. Everything's changing for Ari O'Leary!* I imagined pizza for dinner. A dog of my own. I really wanted a dog."

Toot nodded.[12] And another pang of guilt zipped through Ari's chest: Toot didn't just miss his family. He missed his pet pig. Ichabod—Sal had called him. Ichabod was Toot's buddy.

---

11 **#82:** The Comforter: Smells of dog breath and a well-worn sneaker. Intended to feel like a hug, though it permeates the air with stink.
12 **#47:** The Defensive-Offensive: A toot used by Toot that creates an invisible, yet rancid, cloud of protection around those he loves.

"The lady took me to an old, crumbly house just outside the city," Ariana said. "And I never saw her again. That's when I began working for Mr. Augustus. He's fully wretched." She shrugged. "But he doesn't hit me or anything. He simply doesn't care if I exist. I could run off tomorrow, and he wouldn't care. I almost have, a time or two. But . . . he promised if I'd help him on this mission, he'd give me some money and turn me loose. I could be on my own then. And I guess that's the best option I have left."

Toot waited patiently for her to go on.

"But don't worry. I won't let anybody hurt you," she said. "And anyway, Sal was the first friend I'd had in years. Maybe the best friend I've had, ever. He's wonderful, you know?"

Toot nodded and smiled, dimple-deep.[13]

"He's smart and sarcastic. Real funny. Just a genuinely cool guy. And I betrayed him so big. Like, bigger than big. So I'll take care of you, is what I'm saying. I'll make sure you're settled back in with your family. And then I'll finally be free to see the world."

----

13 **#133**: The Brotherly Love: A toot puffed on the occasion when Toot wants one of his brothers, or will wait for one of his brothers, or just wants to share his love for his brothers. Smells a bit like grilled cheese, a bit like garlic, and a lot like sports gear forgotten in a plastic bag for a week.

Toot patted Ari's hand.

"I don't deserve friends anyway," she said. "That's plain and true. Augustus is wrong in so many ways, but on that matter he's right. I'm nothing to nobody. I've never been wanted. And soon enough, I'll get to be somebody else, maybe. I just dream for now. I sit out here on a big, wide ocean and dream."

Toot cuddled close, and Ari looked out the window, out to the shore, where Cheese Breath's dark form moved toward the villa. He was an inkblot, fanning and fading, heading toward people she had only ever seen from a distance. The woman, she knew, had been involved in the carnival. And involved in everybody's business. She didn't look very nice.

In the palm tree above a small villa sat a mechanical squirrel. The squirrel zoomed in with his camera-eyes and began filming an interaction between an old man in a dark coat . . . and a woman wearing huge sunglasses.

"Augustus," the woman said, crossing her arms. "I'm glad you're here. I'm sorry things didn't work out on the mainland. I'm sure you intended to meet with me before running away."

"The deal is in place," said the old man. "Help

me make sure the Problim children do not destroy the fountain, and I'll give you access to some of the water."

"Half of the water," Desdemona said. "You're not the only one with great plans for the future."

Augustus nodded. "And your father? Is he prepared to help us? I spoke to him a few days ago and he seemed . . . hesitant."

Desdemona stiffened at this. "He is napping now. He's not been himself lately. He's old, Augustus. You know how people get when they age."

"I don't, actually."

Desdemona's eyes swept over him, amazed. "So you're certain it's true. You can't . . . die?"

He smiled, his skin puddling at the corners of his eyes. "I'm one hundred fifty-seven years old now, Mrs. O'Pinion. I'm not immortal. But as long as I don't put myself in harm's way—as long as I have access to the water—I'll be all right."

"I would be afraid to leave my house," Desdemona said, her voice still wavering with disbelief.

"Then what would the point of such a gift be?" he asked. "I am very careful with the life I have been given. The water helps me last. Now I just need a bit more of it. Those stingy Problims have always wanted to keep it for themselves. They've never deserved it."

"They're despicable," Desdemona said, thrilled that someone else clearly hated them as much as she did. "Absolute terrors. Dangerous to other children. Are you sure they'll meet you and take you to the fountain?"

"Oh, I'm certain. I have something they want."

Desdemona chewed on her lip a moment, then quickly changed the subject. As if she didn't want to know the details. Or maybe as if she didn't care.

"Well, that's all that matters," she said. "When they get to you, you signal to me, and we'll all go to the fountain together and take what's ours. I only have one other request."

"I do not negotiate."

"I know, of course. But . . . my daughter is with the Problim children right now. My daughter and my niece. I just want to make sure that the two of them don't get hurt. The Problims brought this on themselves. But my kids are innocent."

"I can make no promises," he said, turning to go. "Danger has a price. So does risk. They chose both."

The squirrel noticed a change in the woman's

features. They weren't granite all of a sudden—something about her mouth softened. "I won't do anything that hurts them. I'll make sure the Problim children are sent to special places far, far away from me. Special homes where they can learn to behave. And then my children will be grounded for all eternity, but . . ."

"Mrs. O'Pinion," Cheese Breath said, taking off his sunglasses and looking at her now, full on. She took two steps back at the sight of his face. "We all do what we must. Meet me in this harbor in two days. The Problim children will be here to lead us all through the mist. And then we will see what happens."

The old man walked away while Desdemona stood silent and stunned on the shore. The squirrel couldn't read her mind. It didn't know what she was thinking. But it had plenty of information now, so it scampered down the tree—a quick flick of silver—and headed back to its accomplices.

The Last Wishbloom

On that same early morning, Sal Problim woke up from a quick nap in the library hull. He hadn't slept all night. Instead, he'd kept his eyes wide while searching for the mist. Thea promised him she'd keep watch, told him that he had to sleep at least a little. They'd all taken turns this way, watching and napping, because nobody can stay awake forever. But he'd tried. At some point, while he was staring out the window of the hull, he'd closed his eyes just for a moment, just long enough to give his body some rest. Someone had pulled a blanket over him while he slept. Sundae, probably. That was nice.

He stretched, turning onto his side, and rolled onto a stinging nettle.

"Mona!" he said with a yelp, flinging the blanket away.

Sal rubbed his eyes and looked out the window. The sun was rising. It was Tuesday—Toot's Day. One more day, he thought. And then he would see Toot and Mama Problim again. The light fell warm and golden over his face.

The sunrise always had—and always would—make Sal think about his mom.

⁓

It was almost a year ago when he last saw her. He'd been tree climbing in the Swampy Woods. The skies had swirled above him that day, churning like an ashy milkshake his siblings might dare each other to drink. Raindrops freckled his face. He felt like a true adventurer as he climbed higher and higher, toes gripping, limbs rough in his hands.

Once he'd climbed as high as he could, Sal had settled onto the crook of a branch and brushed away a cluster of emerald leaves. Hidden beneath them, a tiny, white flower sparkled as if someone had spilled glitter all over its four-petaled face. Sal pulled a small pair of scissors from his sleeve, snipped the bloom, and held it closer to inspect. It looked like freshly fallen snow against his dirty hands.

Pallidus revelare: that's what his science book had called these flowers. But his mother called them something else: Wishblooms.

Sal was a man of science. And like any true scientist, he believed magic was wonderful . . . when it was real. The only way to know for certain, of course, was to experiment.

"I wish for sunlight," Sal said, as he blew on one of the petals. The leaves caught his breath first, turning it to a fine whistle. Then the pale dust swirled up and into the air . . . and landed across his nose.

Glitter-freckles, Sal thought as he sneezed. He opened his eyes to see the same glitter-dust shimmering around him like the first flakes on a winter night. It was a lovely sight, no doubt. But it did not bring out the sun. "So probably no magic here," he declared.

"Just because those flowers have magic inside them doesn't mean they always do magic. All living things have a mind of their own, you know." The words were spoken by a low, feminine voice in the tree beside him. Sal wasn't startled. He'd thought—*hoped*, really—that Mama Problim might be there too.

She had been tucked into the nook of a high branch, long legs dangling from the limb. Her hair was wet, falling over one shoulder. A red flower was tucked behind her ear. Strange, Sal thought, how Mama Problim was like sunshine even when there was no light anywhere.

"Now I believe it," he said. "You're my wish come true."

Mama Problim stretched, climbing into his tree to sit beside him. She draped an arm around his shoulders and smiled. "You have a light inside you too, sweet Sal. You're not just good at growing plants. You can help people bloom too, when you want to."

Sal's heart clenched—not because Mama Problim was being sappy, but because of her timing. She got emotional like this when she was about to leave again.

"I want you to make me a promise," Mama Problim said. "Whenever I'm gone, I want you to keep your siblings together, as long as you can. And I want you to trust them more. Not just trust them to take care of you. But trust them to grow up exactly like they're supposed to."

"I don't follow," Sal said.

Mama Problim nodded. "I think, because you are a man of science . . . it's easy for you to be critical of your brothers and sisters. And of yourself."

"Oh, absolutely," Sal agreed. "How can anybody improve if they aren't criticized?"

A smile played at the corner of Mama Problim's mouth. "I'm not saying you should never be critical or learn how to handle criticism. But do me a favor, okay? When you're about to say something critical—about yourself or someone else—wait . . . just seven seconds. Close your mouth tight and wait. And ask yourself if it's really necessary to say the words . . . or if you should plant a seed instead."

Sal shook his head. "A seed?" His first thought was putting something fun in his siblings' oatmeal every morning that might actually make them grow two feet overnight. But he was sure that wasn't what Mama Problim meant.

"Yes! Call out something good instead. Tell them when you see them being kind or brave or curious or wonderfully weird. Compliments like that are seeds. They stick in a person's heart. They help them grow into the amazing person they were born to be."

Sal sighed. "That's going to be really hard with Mona."

"But if anybody can do it, it's you. And it's so important, Sal. All seven of you have to bloom into your very best and brightest selves. Someday you and your brothers and sisters . . . you'll have to do important things. To do that, you have to keep them together. You have to call out the good in each other. You have to trust each other. Okay?"

"I don't like how you're talking. It sounds like this is a long trip coming up."

"Very long," she whispered. "Very dangerous." She smiled. "The best adventures always are."

Sal held the Wishbloom up between the two of them. Rain fell gently around them, tapping the leaves, tickling their faces.

"I'm going to wish for you to come home safe," Sal said, with a sad sigh. "It makes me sad when we're apart."

"I'm going to wish a life of adventure for you," Mama told him.

She wrapped her hand around his. Together, they blew. The flower whistled softly, and dust swirled up, spreading like glitter in the air all around them.

"Only one petal left," Mama whispered. "Save that one. It's the most magical wish of them all."

Sal had saved it. He would use it for something special someday. Or maybe he would keep it and study it. He pulled the vial from his pocket and held it to the light.

Should he use it now? Use it to wish for safety for his mom? His dad? His baby brother? Or should he trust what Grandpa had said—that Sal and his siblings could do this on their own?

"Please be out there, Mama," Sal whispered. "I've got so much to tell you." He clutched the vial in his hands, and then tucked it back into his pocket.

"Sal!" Thea yelled out, thundering down the steps. "Hurry upstairs!" Her eyes were gleaming, and Sal couldn't tell at first if she was excited or terrified. Until she said: "It's close. The mist, I mean." She shivered. "I can feel it."

21

The Miserable Mist

The library ship suddenly felt very crowded to Sal. In addition to six Problems, the ship now boasted two Wong brothers, the O'Pinion siblings (one of whom would not remove their crown for anything), one fired-up LeeLee Alapo, Violet and her beloved Biscuit, and one sparkly Alabama Timberwhiff. They were all in the captain's quarters (aka the librarian's office). And Sal was trying very hard to focus everyone on the clue. Wednesday was tomorrow. They had to be able to take Cheese Breath to the fountain by *tomorrow*.

"We've made it to this part," Sal said over the noise.

Alabama tapped the paper. "This Miserable Mist . . . it does not sound ideal."

Thea shook her head. "It won't be. We're in peril, Alabama."

"I've been through something similar on my game," Will said, tapping his long finger against his chin. "It's a hard level."

"Well," Mona said, "lucky for us all, the riddle says Monday can get us through this challenge." She paused and grinned. "It's *my* turn to lead," she added, her voice nearly purring with pride.

"How do we know for sure we can trust you?" Sal asked.

Noah nodded quickly. "Excellent question."

Mona turned to Sal slowly. She seemed calm overall. But Sal saw fire in her eyes. "You think *I'm* not trustworthy? Remember the weird girl you befriended in the dump? Remember how she stole your baby brother?"

The room went silent.

And Sal felt embarrassed. It wasn't just his siblings witnessing this spat between him and Mona this time. His friends were seeing it too. And now they knew Sal was responsible for losing Toot. He wanted to yell in Mona's face. She was so difficult! There was no way Mama's seven-second rule applied to her. No way he could plant a seed instead when it came to Mona. Was there?

Sundae stepped forward. "Let's just look ahead to the next step! Sail into the darkness with full hearts!"

Sal didn't speak. He stared at the riddle not really reading any of it, just thinking. Just wondering why this mission suddenly felt so impossible. Thankfully, Frida broke the silence. She climbed onto the table and declared:

> "We've little time left
> till the mist is nigh!
> Fear not, dear friends.
> I'll keep an eye!"

This time, Sal looked at everyone else while Frida spoke. No one was watching her, besides his siblings. No one had turned their attention toward her at all. The sinking feeling Sal felt earlier . . . it suddenly washed over him in a wave as mighty as the mist. And he came to a horrible realization:

People never noticed Frida Problim.

From the first time they'd come into town, nobody even looked at her. And not in a weird way, like when people try to divert their attention on purpose. But in a way like they truly didn't see her. He'd noticed it at the pageant too—the way Mrs. Wong had looked all around when she announced the contestants. Like she didn't even know what a Frida Problim was.

Like Frida wasn't there.

Like she was invisible. Except nobody could hear her either, besides her siblings. Which would make her . . . imaginary?

Mona was realizing it too. She was gauging everyone's reactions. Watching the way Will, Carly-Rue, Violet, Alabama, and the Wong brothers just looked at each other with questions in their eyes. Sal waited until Mona looked directly at him. They didn't have a secret heartspeak language like the twins. But he and Mona were connected in their own weird way. And she was realizing the same thing he was. Sal knew it.

He cleared his throat. "As the pirates say, all hands on deck! A quick tutorial from yours truly, and then it's my sister's turn . . ." He looked at Mona. And gulped. ". . . to guide us through the Miserable Mist!" They all herded out the door, and Sal ran to retrieve the globe from the library hull. When he jogged back to the upper deck, he discovered his entire crew crowded at the rail, pointing over the side.

"That's even worse than I imagined," shouted Alabama. He paused. Then added, "At least I got to be in the pageant before I die."

"I like that positivity!" Sundae said, patting his shoulder.

"Everybody listen to me," Sal shouted. They couldn't solve the riddles or find the fountains unless they got through this part. And he had a feeling that, to do that, they would all have to work together.

"The Miserable Mist will feel like a nightmare," Sal said. "It takes on your worst fears and makes you feel like you're trapped. But there is a way to fight it."

He paced across the deck as he spoke, holding his globe. He'd never felt more like a fearsome pirate. Well—a fearsome but fearful pirate.

Sal pointed to the words on the globe:

"These are Grandpa's instructions," he said. "And he defeated the mist. So he knows. When the mist makes you most afraid," he said, "first, you tell it what you're called. Then you tell it who you are. Practice with me. Tell me what you are called."

"My brother calls me an überdork," Noah Wong said. Alex nodded in agreement.

"That's fine," Sal said. "Tell it that. But then you tell the mist who you are. Like Mona," he said. He took a deep breath. He'd criticized Mona plenty, so that part was easy. "She's often called evil. But . . . she's a good leader, a good friend, and very cunning."

Mona looked confused. "You just gave me three compliments."

Yes, he had. And he didn't feel terrible. He felt okay.

"Or you can use your actual name," he said, turning to his friend. "You're called Alabama. And you are talented, brave, and born to stand out."

Alabama nodded. "That's exactly what I am."

"Frida," Sal said, looking at the little fox. Was

she dimming, just a little? "She's called the fox. She is sly, and quick, and she's a light. She has a personality that shines so bright. Anybody who doesn't see it," he said, looking her in the eye, "is truly missing out."

Her tiny mouth turned up on one side, into a smirk. (Carly-Rue glanced at Will oddly, Sal noticed. But Will just shrugged.)

"Remember that," Sal said. "And we'll defeat this. And then we get to explore the island!"

A celebration shout rose from the entire crew, even as the Miserable Mist ahead billowed larger and darker. It almost looked like it was crawling toward them: a giant spider on the sea.

"It's fine," Sal said, trying to reassure himself. "It's only mist."

"I'm going to barf," said Alex.

"I'm going to fight!" shouted Carly-Rue.

Will tossed his mask onto the deck. "This is so much cooler than my game."

"My turn at the wheel," Mona said to Sal. "You work the sail. And trust me."

"I'm trying," he said honestly.

She scowled at him. "Do you think it's easy to trust you? After what you did?"

You'd have done the same thing! he wanted to shout. But he waited. Seven long seconds. And admitted, "No. I'm sorry."

And then a new look came over his sister Mona— not the kind of fake-innocent look she offered up while she was really plotting where to hide spiders and dig trapdoors. The look in her eyes was something different—something like sincerity. "You don't really have anything to be sorry for," she said. "I would have done the same thing. If you try to trust me, I'll try to trust you. We'll only get through it if we work together."

Sal nearly staggered backward. This thing she'd just given him—this peace offering—was new. This must be what trust felt like. This is what had to happen for them to succeed. Sal knew that from the deepest part of his heart.

"Mona is really leading us through the mist?" Noah asked. His face paled. Clearly, he was remembering Thea and Wendell's birthday party, when Mona had locked him in a room full of spiders.

"We have to trust her," Sal said to the gang. And then he looked Mona in the eye and said, "I trust her. Nothing scares Mona."

"Nothing except conformity," she said with a

sigh. "Even with everyone fighting the mist, we need someone brave enough to drive us through it. That someone is me."

Truly, he probably trusted her more like 77 percent, rather than 100 percent. That was a fine start. Maybe sometimes you really have to decide to believe in something—or someone—before your feelings catch up.

"What you should not trust is the mist up ahead," he told everyone. They still stood huddled in a group, listening. "We can get to the other side of it. Don't forget that when it gets dark: there is nothing truly scary about that mist. If we're brave, we will get through it."

Sal hoped his words would fall like seeds on their hearts. But maybe they weren't. Because Alex slowly flopped down onto the ground, tucked his head between his knees and groaned.

"It's okay, bro," Noah said to his big brother. "I'll take care of you."

"Me too," Sundae said, kneeling beside him. Ichabod nuzzled Alex's face.

Alabama tossed off his sequined jacket and rolled up his sleeves. "Let's fight some fog!"

"Yes," LeeLee shouted. "I need a weapon." She

ran into the office and came back out holding a plunger like a sword. "Come at me and my friends, Mist! I double-dog dare you!"

Violet pulled a jar of Wrangling Ivy from her backpack, opened the lid, and tossed it onto the deck so it would latch onto everyone. Then she strapped Biscuit to her chest and propped her hands on her hips. Ready. She didn't even need her wings to look like a superhero. "I am a Problim too," she whispered. She only needed her heart to hear and believe it.

Wendell and Thea stood tall, side by side, and fist-bumped. And heartspoke, Sal knew. They'd never looked tougher to him. And there was Mona standing at the rail, fearsome as ever. But not in a scary way. In a brave way.

For now—for this second—they were all brave. This was exactly how adventure should feel.

The boat lurched. The gray sky above rolled. Sal felt a cold tangle of ivy wrap around his ankle, and squeeze.

And suddenly, the mist seemed to awaken, to unfurl like a cape and double in size. Then three times. Enough to swallow a boat. Enough to block out the light. It covered the sky.

"It won't hurt you," Sal shouted. But his voice was lost in a sound like thunder.

"Stay close, Problims," Sal cried out, louder.

And they sailed directly into the center of the dark, stormy swirl.

22

Monsters All Around

The Miserable Mist engulfed the library ship.
And suddenly, Sal felt as if he wasn't even on a
boat. He wasn't on anything. He was trying to work
the sail, but the world around him was smoke and
darkness. He couldn't see anyone. Hear anyone.

He was all alone.

"Hello?" he cried out.

Shadowy images of his family staggered toward
him, reaching. This is only mist, he tried to tell himself. But they looked so real. They surrounded him,
called out for him . . . and then, one by one, disappeared with a scream.

Mama.

Papa.

His siblings.

They were hurting. They needed him. They trusted him. But when he tried to grab them, they screamed and became smoke.

You'll be all alone, the mist said to his heart. You are born to be alone. They don't need you. They don't even love you.

Sal felt his knees buckle. Tears fell down his face. He couldn't remember how to get out of this. It was like a dream he couldn't wake up from. Fear was such a suffocating squeeze inside him that he couldn't remember what Grandpa had told him to do.

"I'm Sal," he whispered. That was the first step.

You're worthless, hissed the mist.

"I am Sal PROBLIM!" he shouted. Finally, barely, he heard his family and friends shouting into the mist too. They were swinging at it with their plungers and books.

"Sal!" shouted Mona. "The sail!"

He squeezed his eyes shut tight and pulled. The mist was so thick that he couldn't see Mona, but he could hear her voice. Wendell and Thea stood behind him, heartspeaking, trying to calm the waters just a little—every little bit would help even if Toot wasn't there to make the seven complete.

And then Sal heard a baby crying. He turned and saw a shadowy Toot—crawling along the slick deck, reaching for Sal with his grabby little hands.

You'll never save him, said the mist.

Tears welled in Sal's eyes.

But through blurry tears he saw light. Fiery light. Frida had her arms around him tight. He couldn't feel her. But he could see her . . . shining. Blazing.

"You are the best big brother," she said, looking up into his eyes.

"My shining star.
Scream at the monster, Sal Problim.
Tell it who you are!"

Tell it who you are! That was the other thing. You focus on all the good things about yourself, not the things you're afraid of.

Hands with foggy claws roared up next, and Violet, Noah, and Thea timed a triple-kick that turned it to nothing—all shouting out wonderful things.

"I take great care of my dog!" said Violet. "My dog is my BFF!"

"I'm a skateboard champion!" Noah shouted. "I can peel bananas with my toes!"

LeeLee gave him an odd glance but shrugged. Suddenly a wolf's head emerged from the mist, growling into the girl's face. LeeLee rounded on the beast in the mist, stabbed its smoky eye with the plunger and shouted, "I'm DeLisa Alapo! I'm the best soccer player at Lost Cove Elementary. My parents love me. My dad calls me his shining star. So back down, Mist!"

"My mom says I'm a loner and have zero useful talent," Will O'Pinion said calmly as he looked up into a swirl of gray. "But I create entire worlds."

As he spoke, the mist near him burst like fireworks and fizzled away.

"Go ahead, Sal," Will shouted. "It's . . . kind of fun. Tell it something good and watch it back down."

"I'm a scientist," Sal yelled, toward the little misty version of Toot. Which wasn't really Toot; it was only mist. The same as a bad dream. Absolutely nothing. The image was gone as suddenly as it appeared. "I'm smart. I'm kind . . . mostly. I can make anything bloom!"

The mist parted as far as he could see, billowing off the boat.

"I take care of my family," he said. "I love them. And they love me."

Sundae Problim wasn't even yelling. She and Alex held hands on the side of the ship, whispering.

"You can yell at it!" Sal told her, over the loud swirling in his ears.

"But you don't have to," Sundae said calmly. "Knowing who you are is enough."

Even as fear fanned out inside Sal's chest, he maneuvered the waves. They sailed through the mist. And little by little, the farther they went, the more the fear watered down.

It helped that his friends were close.

It helped that he knew his grandfather, Frank Problim, had sailed this same sea before. He had been a scientist too. He had been afraid of things. And he'd made it.

If he made it, I can make it, Sal thought.

I will make him proud of me.

And finally the last whirl of mist rolled over the boat, and light began to appear ahead—sweet sunlight, beautiful peace.

"We're out of it," Thea said, her voice shaking.

"We're out!" Will echoed. The whole crew erupted in cheers. Frida saluted Sal from the crow's nest. She was absolutely golden with light.

"Mo," Sal said, his voice wavering. "Do you see . . ."

"Is she glowing?" Mona asked.

The fox was like a tiny flame, a beam of light. How was it possible that she was shining?

Sal watched as the Miserable Mist became smaller behind him, drifting like a ghost far out to the sea. Past the terrible fog, the sky was pale blue again. The sun was snuggled behind a cloudy blanket. The waves were playful, not wild.

"Thank you, Frida," Sal said, smiling up at her.

Carly-Rue let out an exasperated groan. "That's it. I can't take it anymore. Who the heck is Frida?!"

23

A Fox Unseen

Alabama Timberwhiff shrugged. "That's just what they all say about things. Haven't you noticed? It's their word for cool. Like, good things happen and the Problims say, 'Yay, Frida!'"

Thea narrowed her eyes. "What?"

Violet cleared her throat, trying to signal Alabama to stop.

"You really don't see her?" Sal asked them. And the group fell oddly silent again. Only the sound of the boat bobbing through the waves rose around them.

"See . . . who?" Noah asked.

Sal knew Noah wasn't being a jerk. Noah was so

cool and kind that Sal knew he was really confused. But . . . how could he be?

"Frida," Mona said, as if it were obvious and the boys were idiots.

"AHOY!" shouted the fox.

None of the stowaways looked up at her.

"They don't see her," Sal said, disbelieving. "Somebody sees her, right?"

The non-Problems on the boat all looked at each other like they didn't know how to answer. Finally, it was Violet who responded gently: "I thought she was an imaginary friend you all made up. And I understand that. I do. I've had all sorts of imaginary friends."

Sundae giggled. "Of course, she's not imaginary."

"She's our sister," Thea said. "You didn't see her the first day when we came into town? She's the little one with the fox hoodie who talks in rhymes. You can't miss her!"

Noah shook his head. "I've never seen her. I've heard you mention her and just didn't know what you were talking about."

Now Frida was beside Sal. He was startled—he hadn't seen the fox sneak back down. But she did this all the time. *The fox was sneaky, sly, and quick!*

But . . . was that because she was invisible?

Or . . . he gulped . . . imaginary?

Frida was nearly in Noah Wong's face. Eye to eye. Her voice was soft, bordering on a sniffle.

"You don't see me.
Look closely,
Stare.
I'm right here in front of you.
I'm not going anywhere."

But Noah never looked at her. He just glanced around nervously.

Frida looked toward Sal. "You see me right?"

None of the other kids heard her. But Sal did.

"Of course," he said. And so did his siblings. That's why she couldn't possibly be imaginary, right? They all saw the same thing, didn't they?

"L-let's take a v-vote," Wendell said. "Everyone who s-sees Frida P-Problim, say aye."

The Problim children (including Frida) raised their hands and shouted: "Aye!"

But everyone else shook their heads. No.

"It's probably just the air out here," Sundae said. "Remember how Grammy said the Miserable Mist makes people see strange things? We must be close enough for it to bother us."

"It's not that," Noah said. "I'm serious. . . . I have never seen her."

Sal looked at Frida, unsure of what to say. But she was staring at the ground now. Even though her fox ears weren't real, just part of the hoodie she always wore, the ears seemed to droop in sadness. She scurried past him, a fiery bolt of orange, and hid behind the mast. The fox had lost her confidence.

The library ship sliced across a calm and endless sea. There was no sign of any island yet. But the Problim children remained hopeful. As they sailed, Sal paid close attention to the fox.

Frida sat beside Thea on one of the steps. Sal kneeled down in front of her and saw—with his own eyes—tears rolling down her face. Surely if she could cry, she was real.

"Hey, fox," he said.

She wiggled her fingers to say hello.

"In the mist, she couldn't see herself," Thea explained. "She couldn't see her hands or her sneakers. Since the other kids can't see her either . . . she's afraid she doesn't exist."

Frida did not speak.

"I saw you," Sal said. "You were as bright as a bonfire in the swamp."

The smallest smile tugged at Frida's mouth.

Should he put his arm around her? He wasn't really into physical touch. It was one of the only things he had in common with Mona. He reached out to touch her—to see—but her eyes flicked up to his.

"What if you feel
that I'm not real?"

His hand stilled in midair. Thea watched him, waiting. But Frida seemed to stare deeper into his eyes, like she was worried.

"If they don't see me,
why should you?
Maybe it doesn't matter what I say,
what I do.
What if one day I start to fade,
like a shadow on a cloudy day?"

A true scientist would reach. Would touch. But . . . he put his arm down.

"Look at me," he said. And she did.

"I see you," Sal said. "I love you. We all do. And when you love someone, they can't fade. It's impossible."

"Promise?" whispered the fox.

"Yes!" Sal said. "I see you. And they will soon enough." He leaned close to whisper. "You are glowing, Frida. You're like . . . a fire. I can't explain it. But whatever power you have, it's going to be amazing."

Her tiny face was a few inches from his when she smiled. And said:

"I see you too, Sal Problim.
I see the powers you've got.
I love you more than a little.
More than a lot."

What if?

What if there were things in this world science couldn't explain? What if they'd all created this sister who suddenly did disappear someday? Separated from one another . . . there was no monster or mist worse than that.

Violet cleared her throat behind him, sending a

186

chirp of static through her mask speaker. "So where is Frida . . . right now?"

"She's beside Thea," Sal said.

Violet looked down. Her eyes were focused on nothing, even though Frida looked directly at her. "Hi, Frida," she said, gently. "I'm sorry I haven't noticed you before. Biscuit and I would like to get to know you though."

Frida's eyelashes fluttered. She looked up at the girl with the helmet and smiled.

"She thinks you're cool," Sal translated to Violet.

Violet shook her head. "It's weird, because I do hear something. I have a theory that the more I listen, the more I'll hear. And eventually I'll see her as easily as I see you. You're not alone, you know," Violet said again, looking in Frida's direction.

She continued, "There are lots of invisible people in the world. It's not just you. We'll help you find a way to be seen."

"Sal!" Mona shouted from the crow's next. "Look!"

Every child—and creature—aboard the boat ran to the rail of the ship. Ahead, they all saw dark land-masses, spread over the sea like lily pads. But one of those masses . . . *one* of them . . . the farthest one . . . sparkled with a thousand shiny gold dots. Like little mirrors reflecting the sunshine. Like an island full of stars. Here and there, a shiny gold dot dropped into the sea.

"That's it," Sal mumbled, afraid to blink, afraid he was dreaming. "That's the Island in the Stars."

24

The Island in the Stars

S al dropped the anchor with a satisfying splash.

"It's bigger than I imagined," Thea said, looking out at the expanse before them. White sand rose up from the sea and disappeared into foliage that reminded Sal a little bit of a jungle. Which was odd. The coast could get hot, *really* hot, but this was more like the kind of island you'd see farther south.

"M-maybe it is m-magic," Wendell said, as if he could read his brother's mind.

"Maybe the fountain feeds it," Sal said with a nod, proud—at first—of this realization. Then dread settled in. If the fountain did feed it, that meant every tree, bush, and flowery branch had potential to bite.

Or worse.

After a lengthy conversation, LeeLee decided to stay on the boat with the animals to guard it. "Don't worry about any little thing," she said, as a smile stretched across her face. "I got this." And they knew she did.

The Problims, the other stowaways, and Violet decided to tackle the island and, hopefully, find the fountain. Before they left, Sal quickly passed out the tools on his sleeves—trying to give every person something sharp to fight with.

"What's this for?" Noah asked, as he took a small set of pruning shears. Sal explained the toothy-plant situation, and Noah's face paled.

"Listen," Mona said to LeeLee, "if something happens . . . if we don't make it back . . ."

"We'll find Toot," Leelee said. "We'll get him home. Don't worry about that. But you will get off this island, Mona Problim. There's not a plant in this world meaner than you."

She meant it as a compliment, Sal knew. He hoped she was right.

The children climbed onto a small raft. Sal positioned himself in the front.

"Why are you the leader now?" Mona asked.

"The clue," Sal told her. "The clue says we—Frida, me, Sundae—have the ability to conquer the island. So we'll lead."

"As long as you lead us back out," Noah said. "I told my mom I was staying with the Problems—it's not a lie—" he shouted when his brother's eyebrows rose, "—but she'd be really mad if I didn't come home."

"We'll take care of you," Sal said.

They rowed the raft to the shore, jumping out when they were close enough to pull it onto the squishy sand.

Sweat dripped down Sal's face and stung his eyes. The jacket felt extra hot here in the burning sunlight. He could take it off. But . . . what would he do without it? It didn't just hold his tools. It made him feel safe, in a way. It made him feel unique from the six other amazing minds he lived with.

"What are you waiting for?" Mona asked. "Let's go."

Sal nodded. He looked at Violet. "What does it feel like without your wings?"

She smiled faintly, as if she knew what he was thinking. "When I'm with my friends—with all of you—I feel like I'm wearing them. I think brave comes from the inside, but it comes from your friends too."

"Right," he said with a sigh. "Right."

And he shrugged out of the jacket. At least one person gasped. Everyone stared.

Sal felt weirdly exposed. Like he might as well have just turned his heart inside out even though it was only a jacket. Yes, he felt lighter without his tools. But he wasn't sure if he liked the feeling.

Sal cleared his throat. "I don't, uh, need it," he told them. But he was really trying to reassure himself. With only one tool in his hand—a long pair of pruning shears—he turned to look to his siblings.

"Oh," Thea said, surprised. "You look . . . different. Are you sure—"

"It's fine," Sal said hopefully. It's not like his jacket was a baby blanket or something. He could do things without it. "Wendell will hold the witch right behind me," he said, changing the subject, "so we can protect him." The crew (minus LeeLee) gathered around Sal in the sand. "Mona and Thea and everybody else can guard us from the back."

Wendell's eyes widened. "M-Mona is walking b-behind me?"

"Truce until we have Toot," Mona said. Then more quietly, she added, "But once we get the baby back, all bets are off."

Sal looked down at Frida, who stood beside him. She wasn't talking much. A zing of panic ripped through his chest. Did she seem more . . . see-through? Or was he just worried? The look on her face was different. He was sure of that much.

"Ready, fox?" he said softly. "I'm going to need you."

"Ready to help.
Ready to go.
If you can't see me . . .
let me know?"

"I see you," he told her again. "Just stick with me."

"Wendell," Thea asked, reaching to bump his fist. "You ready?"

He held out the water witch and nodded. This time, he was confident. "Y-yes."

Together, the Problim children and their friends stepped into the thick, tangled forest.

"Hey, crew," Violet said softly. "Do you hear that?"

"What?" Sal asked.

"Nothing," Violet said. "I don't hear any birds or creatures or anything. Just the ocean. Is that normal?"

"It is weirdly quiet," Sal said. "And where are the stars that were sparkling?"

"We're about to find out," Mona said.

They walked through dense brush, palms forming a leafy canopy overhead. Sweat dripped down their foreheads as they tied back their hair, pulled up their sleeves, and swatted away the mosquitos biting their arms. They felt the brush crackle beneath their wet sneakers. They pointed out the occasional lizard hidden in the swirls of the tree bark. So far, so good, Sal thought. Or maybe not. Why weren't the birds singing? Why was it so quiet now?

And when would Frida, Sal, and Sundae have to use their super-sibling powers to do stuff?

"Steady on," Wendell said, the witch extended. "I can feel it p-pulling. It's so w-weird, you guys."

And then a glint in the high trees caught Sal's

eye. It was an owl—sort of. But like the squirrel and the bird, it was mechanical. Other than the plume of purple feathers above the owl's eyebrows, it was made of gears and shifts.

"Stop," Sal said, his voice hovering above a whisper. But everyone had heard him. They grouped up behind him, and looked to the tree where he pointed.

"It's one of Grandpa's mechanical creatures!" Thea said. "That's what we must have seen shining! It looked like there were so many of them. Where did the rest of them go?"

"Something's not right," Sal said. He couldn't put his finger on it, but the bird . . . it wasn't doing anything. Just staring.

A whirring *zzzzz* and the bird suddenly spread its metal feathers wide and dove.

Directly toward them.

"Move," Sal screamed, shoving Wendell out of the way, and the bird plunged into the ground, leaving a skull-sized dent in the dirt.

Then the woods began rustling, moving, as if the whole earth was coming awake.

"I don't like that sound," Thea said.

"It's just nature," Sundae offered. "Glorious, wondrous—"

"Time to run," Mona said calmly, shoving them all ahead of her. Sal looked back to see hundreds of glinty lights—from the beaks of lots of metallic birds—hurling at them through the woods.

The children took off in a herd, thundering through the low brush and around trees.

WHACK! One of the robots hit a tree trunk beside them. Hard.

"That could have been my head!" Thea shouted, just as Sal tackled her. A robotic grasshopper shot past the place where Thea's eye would have been.

"Grandpa outdid himself with these traps!" Sundae shouted, gasping for air. "What fun!"

"This is fun?" Will asked.

Carly-Rue ran up beside him and kicked a whirring robo-bug into space. "Super fun."

"Whoa!" Mona ducked to the ground, and Wendell stopped to help her up back up. Sal caught the glint of a mechanical hawk diving for the two of them. He reared his long pruning shears back behind his head like a baseball bat, like he was ready to hit a home run. With a loud CLANG, he knocked the hawk toward the ocean.

"G-good hit," Wendell shouted, scrambling past him. "Let's g-go, M-Mo! What are you d-doing?"

Mona had crouched under a tree. She was fishing through her backpack. The rest of the crew had darted behind trees too, leaning out occasionally to whack a creature to outer space.

"This is no time for a prank, Mona!" Sal shouted, jumping behind a nearby tree.

"Is it a time for Bloomfizz?" Mona asked. She tossed a bottle to Sal.

He grabbed it, glancing quickly at the faded label. "You took this from the hotel room?"

Mona nodded. "Obviously. That drink made people fly. I'd intended to save it for later. Hide it in your breakfast one morning. But it could be useful."

Sal had to admit . . . this was brilliant.

"Bust them open on the trees," Sal instructed, tossing bottles to his siblings. "Take a drink, pass it to the person beside you, and then get ready. According to the internet, Bloomfizz makes you airborne for three minutes."

"Not to be the fun police," Thea shouted, ducking behind a tree. "But this drink made people fly forty years ago. It's been sitting around for a long time. It might not work at all now. Or it might shoot us to the moon."

"Violet," he said, running over to her, "I know

you can't take your mask off. Put your arms around my and Mona's shoulders, and we'll carry you."

"We're going to fly?" Violet asked. "Like, fly for real in the sky?"

Sal nodded. "No wings necessary this time. But when it wears off, I'll bet we'll hit the ground pretty hard. Mona's right though; it's the only way to get away from them."

Violet stretched her arm around his shoulder as Mona scrambled over beside them. All around, the crew tried to swig Bloomfizz and whap mechanical creatures away.

WHACK!

A robo-rabbit cannonballed into the tree right above Sal's head. Mona gave it a mighty soccer kick back toward the sky.

"Drink up!" Sal shouted.

While birds with extra-sharp beaks clattered and smashed into the trees, the children guzzled the rest of the bottles. Sal tasted sugar water and dust, plus a faint floral something. He felt like he was drinking an old book, or a gross bottle of perfume. He swallowed with a grimace on his face.

"No wonder they discontinued this stuff," Thea said.

"You okay leading?" Sal asked Wendell.

Wendell nodded. And then his eyes went wide as he floated up off the ground. "Wh-whoa!"

"Okay," Sal said, remembering the advertisement he'd seen on the Isle of St. Maria. "On three, everybody jump, and move your legs like you're running."

"This is so fun!" Sundae shouted, grabbing Alex's hand.

They all hunkered down, ready to launch, while wild robo-creatures screeched past their ears.

"One!" Sal shouted. "Two! Three!"

He jumped, and his legs tread the air. And it turned out—thankfully—running in air is much faster than running on land. Sal, Violet, and Mona bolted above the trees. Then they flew, zooming over the forest canopy. The robo-animals followed in a shiny horde.

"Faster!" Wendell shouted, pumping his legs on warm air.

They whizzed past trees and plants and through a flowery dusting of ivy. Sal looked back, relieved to see they'd gained some ground on the creatures. (Because it's not like robots get tired.) But, as he feared, the Bloomfizz didn't last long. The Problim children began to slow down—despite their better efforts—floating lower and lower toward the ground. Toes touched, then feet. And then they were running through the jungle again.

"S-STOP!" Wendell yelled. "Get d-down!"

The children all slammed to the ground. Sal was caught in a tangled web of arms and legs at the very edge of a grassy cliff. Far below them stretched a wide canyon with a rushing river zigzagging down the center.

"You don't have any more Bloomfizz?" Sal asked Mona. "How do we get down there?"

Before anyone could answer, Wendell already had his eyes closed . . . and the river water was rising.

"He's going to bring it up here," Thea said, "so we can ride it like a waterslide."

"No way," Alabama mumbled.

"I told you!" Noah whispered. "They're magic!"

The Problems reached for each other—reached for Wendell—begging the river to rise faster.

"I hope lifting the river doesn't hurt the environment," Sundae said nervously.

Apparently, the river had no intention to do so. The water stayed together, stretching like taffy in one solid piece, rising toward them. The rest of the world around them seemed unmoved.

But the buzzing sound was growing louder behind them. The creatures were coming.

"C'mon, Wendell," Sal said, anxiously. He lifted his shears like a baseball bat again. Mona, Thea, and Sundae did the same. Frida the fox stood beside her brother, watching the woods.

The wild roar of the river was getting closer—it was moving higher—but not fast enough.

This would be bad, Sal knew.

They couldn't fight them all off. Someone was going to get hurt. He saw a sparkle in the trees, a shimmer of sharp feathers and beaks and claws. They braced for the feeling of a thousand robotic animals smashing into them.

"NO," said the fox.

It was the shortest poem she'd ever uttered. And suddenly, the same as last night on the beach, something about Frida seemed to glow. First, she was barely beaming. Seconds later, she was blazing.

"Is she trying to get their attention?" Mona yelled to Sal.

He shook his head, unable to look away from the fox. "I think she feels protective. That's when she shines, when she's taking care of her family."

Frida walked around in front of her brother, and stretched her hands out toward the creatures.

"I'm Frida Mae Problim.
Not hidden,
I'm here!
If you want to see me,
I'm perfectly clear!
I'm as visible as I choose to be.
My family means the world to me!"

And then she screamed and fire burst from her tiny hands toward the woods, creating a mighty wall of heat. The robotic animals sizzled as they slapped against the fire, then hurriedly flew and hopped and bounced in the direction from which they'd come. Away from the flames.

Away from the children.

Friday's child is loving and giving, Sal thought; she loved so much that it was a fiery presence inside of her soul. They'd never seen her use her fire before this. In fact, if anything, Frida was so clumsy, Sal was half-afraid she'd burn the woods down any minute. But she didn't. Her love made her passionate, and that passion gave her real flames shooting from her fingertips. She stood strong, ears pointed.

"Let's go!" Wendell shouted, as the river water finally climbed to the cliff's edge to meet them. One by one (with the witcher going first), they slid down the swirling waterslide Wendell had created, down into the canyon hundreds of feet below.

Only Sal and Frida were left. Animals were still bouncing off her fire wall. Sal reached out, and touched her shoulder. Well . . . he touched where her shoulder should be. Did she feel like air? Or was she there? He'd hugged his sister a million times in his life. He'd never noticed her *feeling* invisible.

But he'd also never seen her shining like this. She was capable of this cool thing. An amazing ability she was just growing into. Somewhere in the back of his mind, Sal thought about how easy it would be to start campfires now. He couldn't feel her. But he could feel the heat from her fire. The heat of her heart.

"On three," he said. "Let go, and fall back into me.

"One, two . . ."

"Three!" she shouted.

And she did fall back, with her arms open wide. And they fell backward together—Sal and the mightiest fox he knew—onto the waterslide that spun them down into the canyon. As the flames above disappeared. As the sky grew farther and farther away.

25

Saturday Sees Clearly

The Problims sat on the bank of the river. They were dripping wet and a little confused.

"We came from up there," Mona said, pointing to the canyon walls above. "And we got here alive thanks to Wendell's waterfall and Frida's blazing fire wall. . . ."

Mona glanced at her little sister, the fox. Frida sat silently stunned, a slow smile spreading over her face.

"Mama always said Frida had a special fire inside her," Sal said. "It just took a while to come out."

Thea applauded. "Bravo, foxy!"

Violet tilted her head sideways, looking in Frida's

direction. "Do you call her fox because she wears fox ears on her jacket? 'Cause I think I see her. Sometimes. In a blurry way. She's getting more clear to me, just like I thought!"

"I want to see her," Noah said glancing around hopefully. His face was smudged with dirt and sweat, and he'd tied a bandana around his forehead. "I'll keep looking, I promise."

"Same," Alabama said. "Glad you're here, Miss Fox."

Frida curtsied toward him.

"Thank you dearly.
I see you clearly.
I think you're very kind."

Will and Carly-Rue said nothing. They leaned against each other's shoulders, worn out. But they looked for her too. Sal wondered if their faces had always looked this nice and open. He'd always assumed they were rotten because they were O'Pinions. Which, really, had made him as terrible as Desdemona, hadn't it?

Maybe it's impossible to truly see a person until you get to know them.

"Well, I never thought she was imaginary," Mona said. "The rest of them will realize it too. Just wait."

"Glad that worked out," said Wendell, as he stood up and dusted off his pants. Sal felt a rush of pride for his brother. He heard confidence in his voice. Wendell looked as natural out here on this strange, wild island as he did reading in the kitchen window back home.

"Well done," Sal said. Wendell nodded to him. He didn't speak, but he didn't have to. They didn't have a secret heart language, like Wendell and Thea. But brothers get each other too.

"Enough group bonding," Mona said. "Let's keep tracking."

"Lead the way, twinsies!" Sundae shouted.

Wendell held the stick out, like a knight holding a sword. "S-straight ahead. A-along the bank."

He looked to Thea. She rested her hand over her heart. There was no map for this part. Now she had to follow the one inside her heart, a map she was still learning to trust. Still learning to use. Thea's element was magnetism, which was easy enough when it came to bolted doors and rusty locks. But the magnetism that unlocks the world . . . that took patience to figure out, surely.

"What does it feel like?" Sal asked. "When you use your power?"

"It still feels like opening a door," Thea said. "But the door is down deep somewhere, clasped over the heart of the earth. It's locked, so you have to work with it. In my imagination I reach down and down . . . gently . . . and undo that lock. And I think the world knows its secrets are safe with me. It's like I can feel movement below me. And that's what I follow."

"That's pretty incredible," Sal said.

Thea nodded, agreeing with him. They talked as the party moved. "Does it feel that way for you?"

"Maybe a little," Sal said. "When I close my eyes, I feel like the ground I'm standing on is an eggshell. And something—all kinds of wonderful somethings—are trying to burst free. I help them. I'm convinced some of the most beautiful things in the entire world just need a little encouragement to break free."

"That's a nice thought," Thea said. And they both looked at the fox walking along beside them. Frida looked at her hands, palms up. Then she spread her hands wide and turned them out in front of her. Tiny flames flicked from her fingertips and she giggled.

They were getting stronger, Sal realized. All of them. Maybe even Toot?

The group traveled together along the riverbank of the canyon, leaving sneaker prints on the muddy shores.

"Uh-oh," Thea said, after a time.

Sal, who'd been watching for Frida's footprints (there were none), looked up. His eyes widened.

"Well, Saturday's child," Mona said, clamping his shoulder. "This is all you."

26

Saturday's Child

The riverbank had trailed into dense foliage again. And now they stood in front of a wall of ivy. A cage of ivy. Upon first glance, Sal thought the ivy was trembling in the breeze. But he could see now the ivy was actually chomping. Every tiny leaf had a set of pointy teeth.

"Not again," Sal said with a sigh.

"Want us to help you cut through?" Thea asked.

Sal shook his head. "That'll take too long. Plus, we'd all get bit. There are so many leaves."

He hated asking for help . . . but time was running out. "Wendell. When you made the water rise, what did you do?"

"I-it sounds crazy, b-but I talked to it. I-inside my m-mind."

"It helps if you put your hand over your heart," Thea said. "You can feel the earth. I don't know how else to explain it."

Sal closed his eyes. He pressed his hand against his chest. There was no vest of tools covering it now. He felt his heart, wildly beating. His breath, falling and rising.

And then it was as if he could feel what was happening underground, all around him. Animals tunneling. Roots tangling. He could feel plants stretching deeper and deeper into the earth. Water running through veiny threads into full-bloomed life. He spoke to the world as if it was just him in his garden:

"I need a path," he said. First, he looked at the ground. Then the treetops. Which part of the earth do you focus on when you're trying to talk to it? "Could you help me?" The ivy began to tremble and slither, slipping against itself and tangling into new shapes.

"It's working, S-Sal!" his brother called out.

Sal closed his eyes harder, focusing all of his mental strength on that wall.

"Wow," he heard Thea say.

"Oh, Sal," Sundae said. "This is extraordinary. You are extraordinary."

His heart bloomed at the words. He wanted to argue at first. To remind her that he wasn't. But then . . . he waited seven seconds. Because she'd gone and planted a seed too. And it had worked. Her words did make a difference; he could feel it. Sure, he was part of the reason Toot was gone. But he was also helping bring him home. That was something.

A hand clapped down on his shoulder—Mona's hand—and his eyes shot open.

The ivy wall no longer existed. It had tangled and reshaped itself into a swinging bridge stretched across a deep gorge. It lead them to more land.

"Not bad," Mona admitted.

"Now we just have to walk over it," Thea said, glancing down below.

"You can do it," Sal reminded her. "You can do anything. Wanna take my hand?"

"Maybe we should all hold hands," Thea suggested.

"You heard her," Alex said, reaching for Sundae. "We have to hold hands."

Sundae stared at Alex and he stared at her. Sal

was surprised that bubbly, cartoon-hearts didn't shoot out of their eyes.

"Good grief," Sal mumbled. Did crushing on someone make everyone this incapable of focusing on catastrophe? If so, he would never ever—*under any circumstances*—fall in love. Or even in like. Or have a crush. Or get crushed. Whatever.

Sal went first, settling his shoe onto the bridge. It wobbled under his weight. "It's sturdy," he called behind him. "It just doesn't look that way."

"It l-looks like s-something Mona would m-make and d-dare me to w-walk ac-cross."

Mona sighed. "Like the time in the swamp, when I made a bridge of hay over the alligator nest. The good old days."

They made their way across somehow, slowly, holding on to one another, never looking down. Safe on the other side, Thea let out a burst of air she'd been holding for the length of the bridge. "Thank goodness that's over. Now where, Wendell?"

He didn't answer. Wendell stood off to the side, his back to everyone. The water witch extended toward a dark cave.

"Is that it?" Sal asked.

Wendell shook his head. "I don't th-think so.

But there's w-water in there. Some k-kind of water. Grammy Payne said there was "enchanted water" on this island. But this isn't the b-bunny ear c-cave. Sh-should we look, j-just to make sure?"

Sal nodded. "But let's be quick. We've got to get Cheese Breath back here."

"T-take the lead, M-Mona," Wendell said, waiting for her to waltz to the front of them all.

"Gladly," she said at first. But within a few minutes—after she'd paused and caused them all to trip twice—she felt differently. "This is . . . weird," she said, her voice echoing off the walls of the cave.

"Weird how?" Sal asked.

Mona let out an exasperated sigh. "I just . . . I can't see as well as usual. I mean, this is . . . a different kind of dark. What a perfect hiding spot this must be."

Sal traced his fingers along the cold walls. They were slimy and wet, vibrating with life. Another sudden stop. Sundae yelped as she tripped over one of her siblings and hit the ground.

"Stop stopping!" Thea shouted. "We're like dominoes!"

"I can't see!" Mona reminded her. "I don't know what's wrong."

"Sundae!" Sal shouted. "You can bring the light!"

"Oh, I'm so excited!" Sundae cried. "Okay, hand on my heart, speak to the sun. Dear sun, I adore you. I adore your warmth, and I need your help—"

The light of the sun—who was as impatient as Sal, apparently—answered quickly. First, they felt its warmth. Then they squinted against the brightness as the light flooded corners, illuminating the stone walkway in front of them.

"Good teamwork," Sundae said to Mona, settling in beside her as they walked deeper. They emerged into a cavern full of pools.

"Are these all enchanted?" Thea asked. "They must be! They're so bright!"

"I don't think they're all fountains of youth," Sal said, fishing through his backpack to find one of Grandpa's old journals. "Remember the picture we saw of this pool? He called it 'The Lake of Dreams.'"

"The slide was titled 'The Hub,'" Mona added. "Whatever that means."

"It looks beautiful," Sundae cooed.

"Nobody touch it," Sal said. "There's no way to know it's not dangerous. Beautiful things usually are." He glanced at Mona. She shrugged.

The pool seemed to glow, lit somehow from

underneath. And the water rippled as if someone invisible was skipping rocks across the surface. Sal stared at it, unblinking. He wanted to step into it, though he couldn't explain why. He'd never been a good swimmer. But the water was magnetic, pulling him closer . . . closer . . .

A yelp from Thea pulled Sal out of his daydream.

"Thea?" He didn't see her. His siblings and friends were all looking around, as if they'd snapped out of a sudden stupor.

"W-where is she?" Wendell asked frantically.

She called out again.

Sal ran down the dark cavern toward the sound of her voice, tripping and grabbing the slimy walls. He rounded a corner . . . and saw light. And Thea, still running.

"It's not just a cave! It's Grandpa's lab!" she shouted as her sneakers pounded the ground. "Grammy Payne said he had a secret lab on the island! Remember? That's got to be what this is. . . ."

Her voice trailed off as she rounded a dark bend, and a tremor of terror bolted through Sal. Had she fallen? Had she found the quicksand pit? His siblings were rushing around him, toward the darkness.

As Sal rounded the same bend of the rocky maze, he was relieved to see Thea standing very still up ahead of him. There was also a small laboratory up ahead, with a chair pulled up to a table.

And there was someone sitting in that chair.

Mama Knows Best

The figure at the table turned slowly to face them.

In this darkness, it could be anyone—it could be Cheese Breath or Desdemona or someone they hadn't even met yet. Someone else trying to find the treasure. Surely the world had more siblings of seven, more people accomplished at finding things.

"Sal?"

The sound of her voice dropped like an anchor into his chest. The human heart is chaos; he knew. A big storm of questions and worries. But then someone you love says your name and it anchors you. You're suddenly safe in the wind.

"Mama?" Sal whispered. He heard the soft gasps of his siblings and Violet. He heard Sundae whispering to the sunlight until it flooded the room, gently, shining over Mama's face. She was an angel in the darkness, sparkling in that special way she always had. And before Sal's mind had time to register what his feet were doing, he was racing toward her. And her arms were around his shoulders.

His siblings followed, crowding in to hug her tightly. They all had so many questions. They shouted all at once:

"Did Cheese Breath let you go?"

"Is T-Toot with you?"

"Are you okay?"

"Is Frida invisible?"

"Where is P-Papa? D-did he f-find you?"

"Did you find the fountain?"

"Are you their mom? Can you call my mom?" Noah sighed. "Gosh it's nice to see a real adult."

"Stop," Mama said softly. "One at a time." Her eyes scanned the tops of their dirty heads, counting. "Where is Toot?"

"He's with you," Sal said. "Cheese Breath captured you and Toot and probably Papa too."

Something registered in Mama's mind then, and the love in her eyes changed to concern (which is a feeling no less full of love, but includes worry too).

"Problims pile up," she said calmly. "Tell me everything. Because I have some things to tell you too."

Sundae softened the sunlight in the cave laboratory, which sparkled against some blue, pebbled fragments in the walls. The Problim children and their friends gathered around Mama. She looked tired, Sal now realized. Beautiful—she always looked beautiful—but tired too.

"First, Frida," Mama settled into the rolling seat near a lab table. She waved for Frida to come close. The fox did so, gladly. "Frida is as real, wonderfully real, as you want her to be. And she's as real as she wants to be."

"I'm certainly real," Frida said.
"I can cry.
I can feel.
I love and I laugh.
What's more real than that?"

221

"Exactly," Mama said. "So yes, she's real. That's not the issue here."

Frida the Fox crossed her arms over her chest and smiled proudly.

"Um, that's actually a terrible resolution," Sal said. "We need a concrete answer!"

"You don't always get those in life," Mama told him. "Or science."

Sundae shrugged. "She's real then. That's all that matters."

Sal groaned.

"Now, Cheese Breath is the very old man, right?" Mama Problim asked. They nodded. The sigh she let out sounded very close to a laugh.

"His breath does smell a lot like cheese. His real name is Augustus Snide. This is how your father tells the story: many years ago—when your grandfather Frank was a boy—Augustus Snide was a professional adventurer and treasure seeker. Kind of like Major and I are now."

The Problims all looked at one another.

"Is that how Grandpa knows him?" Sal asked.

"That's how both of your grandfathers know him," Mama answered with a catch in her voice. "Your grandpa Frank was a boy when he met

Augustus Snide. The man came to Lost Cove in search of a tree that would lead to the fountain of youth. He was a charmer, your grandpa said. A funny and vibrant man who told marvelous stories."

"But," Thea added, looking at her friends, "Cheese Breath was totally evil. Even before the water, he was the villain."

Mama nodded. "He promised your grandfather and the rest of the Problim siblings great wealth if they helped him on his search. Stanley, my dad," she smiled at Violet, "was one of their best friends. So he knew it was all happening."

"Money," Carly-Rue said with a groan. "It makes people do such stupid things."

"Money is good sometimes," Mama told her. "Grandpa and his siblings didn't need stuff—they were perfectly happy the way they were. But the Problim children believed it was their chance to help out their parents. Their family was wonderful, you know. But very poor. And money, regardless of how good or bad it is, gives you access to things. Help, if you need it. Food, if you don't have it. It can ruin people, sure. But there's no doubt it can also help if you use it the right way."

"And the water," Sal said. "They probably wanted

the water too, right? They didn't know it was bad. . . ."

"Right," Mama answered Sal's question. "Frank Problim and his siblings—and their friend Stan—found it first. Stanley didn't go into the cave; only the Problims did that. And they realized it wasn't what it seemed because of the plants in the cave. They tried to tell Cheese Breath. But he would not be persuaded. They gave him one jar, to see, they said. They told him to throw it on a plant and see. But he guzzled it, apparently. The old man didn't feel the change that came over him. He demanded access to the full fountain. And I believe, even then, Stanley began to wonder if the Problims were lying—if they just wanted the water for themselves."

"So they had to destroy it," Sal said.

"Yes, and they did," Mama Problim told them. "But your grandpa believed Cheese Breath would come back someday. Especially once he realized—as you did—that another fountain existed out here. And he also believed, once it became obvious there would be seven of you, that you'd be the ones to smash it once and for all. Your dad agrees. He says it's the Problim family way but . . . I worry."

"My aunt is after it," Violet said, then tilted her

head slightly. "Your sister, I mean. I suppose you're my aunt too?"

Mama Problim nodded and beamed. They looked alike, Sal realized. They even reminded him of each other, a little bit. He wondered if this was a tiny part of the reason he'd liked Violet from the start—because she had a familiar kindness in her eyes. Because she reminded him of the most lovely person he'd ever known.

"I am indeed. My sister believes it's all a cover-up so we can keep the fountain for ourselves. It's not. You know that, and I do too. I've looked at all of Frank's research now. And I know he was telling the truth. He was a little bit crazy," she said with a smile. "But in a wonderful way."

"*Was* telling . . . ," Sal said. "*Was* crazy . . ." A ripple of horrible sadness rolled through him.

Mama looked into his eyes. She was not one to look away from sadness. Somehow, Sal knew what she would say even before he told her.

"Your grandpa Frank left Lost Cove and began putting things in place—safety measures so no one would find the fountain except for all of you. Riddles that would make it difficult for anybody else to discover it. When he told your father and me, we understood at first. We're adventurous too! He found us when we were in Andorra. He was excited about everything ahead of you. But it all made me nervous. I thought he meant you'd have this big adventure some-day. Not so soon. But he said he knew you were ready. And he stayed up late telling us about the adventures he'd had all over the world, all the while writing these clues for you. He felt like time was running out. Like someone bad was closing in on the fountain, and it was time for you to make your move. And then . . ."

"And then?" Sal echoed.

"He fell asleep one night," Sal's mother said. "And he woke up in the Great Forever."

"He died?" Sal asked, his voice cracking, which was embarrassing, but he didn't care right now.

"Do you remember how the Narnia books end?" his mother asked. "The last words say there is a chapter one of a greater story. I think that's what happened. Yes, he left this world and that means dying. But I also think it means he's having an adven-ture somewhere else. He was never afraid of dying, you see. I am not afraid of dying. I am afraid of not living a life of adventure and bravery and curiosity.

He was very happy. He was not afraid. He loved you all so much."

Sal thought the ceiling was dripping onto his chest and then realized it was his tears. Deep down, he'd believed all along Grandpa Problim was hiding out in a cave somewhere—just like this one—making riddles and helping them along. But he wasn't there. He'd slipped away.

"At first, I tried to finish his plan," Mama told them. "Tried to get this going so you could find the fountain and finish it off. But then I realized how hard it would be. That's why I left the note for you in the Pirates' Caverns. Along with the Truth Teller Drops; that's a formula your grandpa gave your dad years ago. He said no adventurer should leave home without secret drops."

She laughed sadly and continued, "I wanted to try to do all of this for you, but this is as far as I can get. I found this cave a few days ago. I opened the door and that gold bird just zoomed out of here like it had been trying to get out for weeks."

Sal glanced at Mona. He'd seen her fiddling with her watch right before the bird cannonballed into the boat. She simply gave him a shrug.

Mama sighed. "I don't doubt how strong you are, but you're only children. It seemed like a heavy burden to bear."

"I'm sorry I lost Toot," Sal said.

"We lost Toot," Mona said, surprising him. "All of us."

"And we'll all find him," Mama said. "At least Cheese Breath lied about having me and your father," Mama pointed out. Her eyes glimmered in a sappy, lovey way when she mentioned Papa Problem. "Yes, I worry too. But don't doubt how strong Toot is. You told me he's sending you signals. I believe Toot and your papa are out there and safe. We'll all be back together soon."

Her words gave him a rush of confidence. Mama Problem was a natural seed-planter.

"I wish we could have seen Grandpa again," Sundae said. "We didn't have him for very long."

"That's so hard," Mama Problim said, and Sal could see her heartbreak shining through her eyes. "I'm sorry, my sweet Problims."

Wendell and Thea were standing beside each other, shoulder to shoulder. Thump-bumping, Sal knew. Comforting each other with their secret language. Comforting each other in a way that you can when your sibling also happens to be your best friend. He wouldn't have minded a hug just then. Part of him wanted to go punch the wall of the cave—which was weird. Sal never wanted to punch anything. Part of him wanted to fall into Mama Problim's chest and cry.

But he was the leader of this mission. So none of those things were appropriate, were they? Sal took all of his feelings and smooshed them deep into his heart. All except anger. Anger was good. He wanted to be angry when he found Cheese Breath.

"We're close," Sal said, clearing his throat and thinking of something else. Anything else. "We need to find a rabbit-shaped cave."

Sal pulled the clue from his jacket to show her.

TOGETHER IS THE WAY TO REACH THE RIGHT END,
WHERE A RABBIT-SHAPED CAVE CALLS YOU TO DESCEND.

"We saw it in Grandpa's slides," Sal said. "That's where we think the final fountain is. And then we'll lead Cheese Breath back over here—somehow— we don't know how yet—get Toot back and, poof. Smash it."

But nobody else was listening to him. They were

huddled together, softly crying. Or talking about Grandpa. As the minutes stretched on they talked about memories they had of him, of his purple jackets and whiskered face, and it was all too much.

His mother reached for his shoulder, but Sal pulled away.

"I need to go plan," he said. But that's not really want he wanted to do.

~~~

Sal climbed out from the cave. He sat on the soft grass and looked up at the sky—at its star-freckled face.

He wanted to shout at it. No, to roar at it. To roar at him. Grandpa had promised Sal they would fish again. He had promised that they'd have adventures together someday. Sal felt betrayed.

I will not see him again, Sal realized. And a feeling he'd never experienced before made his heart feel achy and raw. Like a cut that burns. Like a burn that blisters. He bit down hard on his lip to keep from crying again. The stars blurred in his vision.

"Hey, dude," Will O'Pinion said, walking up behind him. "Can I sit here?"

"I don't care," Sal said, looking up at him. Will

seemed especially tall with Sal this close to the ground. "I don't want to have a heart-to-heart, if that's your mission."

Will settled down beside him, folding up his long, skinny legs and locking his hands around his knees. "That's fine. I just wanted to see the stars." He was quiet for a second. "I used to have this dog I loved. Supernova—Nova for short. She was the best dog. We looked at the stars together. Here's what's crazy, dude—my dog passed away when I was seven years old. I'm sixteen now. So that's been . . . lots of years."

"Nine years," Sal said. So many people couldn't even do simple math.

"Right," Will said. "Nine years. And I think about her every day. And miss her every day."

Sal looked at Will's face expecting tears. But he was smiling.

"How can you be happy?" Sal asked.

"I'm not happy, exactly," Will said. "I wish Nova was here. She'd love this adventure. But I've realized, I guess, that the missing place isn't bigger than the loving place. I love her even more than I miss her, if you can believe it. I feel like she's still watching out for me. I know it sounds silly."

"Nah," Sal said. "I'm sure she is. All dogs go to the Great Forever."

"Yeah, they do," Will said. He said nothing else after that. Just looked toward the sky.

So did Sal.

And then Sal remembered a night many years ago when he was small. So small he only kept one tool clipped to his jacket. Grandpa Frank was in the Swampy Woods, and he picked Sal up, lifting him to his shoulders.

"Why can you feel love but not see it?" Sal had asked, stretching small fingers toward the sky trying to poke, poke, poke a star of his own.

"You can see it sometimes," Grandpa had told him. "Hugs are how we show love."

"Yes, but it seems like something you should see. Like you see water."

"But you don't see air," Grandpa said.

Which was also frustrating. Even then, Sal needed a reason for things. Proof.

"Some of the best things in this world are invisible, my boy. But that doesn't mean they aren't real. Love is real."

"How much do you love me?" Sal asked.

"If my love were a lasso, it'd be enough to rope every star in the sky."

LASSO THE STARS.

That was it! That was the part of the clue Grandpa hadn't finished writing.

AND SAL, DO REMEMBER,
WHEN THINGS SEEM TOO HARD,
EYES TO THE SKY,
AND LASSO THE STARS!

"Whoa!" Sal shouted.

Will jumped up from the ground looking all around. "What? Who is it?!"

"It's not a person," Sal said. "I had an epiphany! Lasso the stars!"

Will just stared. And that was fine. He wouldn't know anything about that phrase, because it belonged to Sal and his grandpa.

Lasso the stars! Between Sal and Frank Problim, it was the same as saying I love you.

Through tears, Sal smiled. Because living with an open heart was so painful. But he was beginning to believe that love was still worth the risk.

"Sal? Will?" The boys turned to see Violet, holding Biscuit. She smiled at them. "Big development in here. Mama Problim . . . Aunt Mina . . . says she knows where to find the rabbit-shaped cave."

28

Villains Converge

In the early morning light of Wednesday, the Problim children, their mom, and their friends stood in front of a large cave that cast a rabbit-shaped shadow. It was the rock formations on top that made the structure look like a bunny. Otherwise it looked like any cave. And yet, Sal knew, this cave had an important secret deep inside it.

"Here's what I think we should do," Sal said. "I think Wendell, Thea, and Mona should go back through the mist and bring the baddies through. They're strong enough to face the mist again."

"I am excited to face it again," Mona clarified.

"The rest of us," Sal continued, "should stay here and wait."

"You're sure it's best to split up?" Thea asked.

"Absolutely," Sal continued. "I don't think Cheese Breath will send anybody else. I don't think there are more villains, but I want to be here just in case. The robo-monsters should be obliterated now, thanks to Frida's flame. The ivy chompers at the bridge won't grow back together before you get through them. I'm only sad I can't see Cheese Breath go through the Miserable Mist. Don't tell him how to fight it. Make him suffer."

"I approve of that plan!" Mona said. "And once we're all back here together . . . we grab Toot and smash this thing."

"I'll be here," Mama Problim said. "This time I can help you."

"Actually," Sal said gently, "you can't. We have to do this on our own. We're the seven."

She opened her mouth to object, but Sal reached out for her hand and said, "Trust me?"

Tears sparkled in Mama Problim's eyes. But a proud smile filled her face. "Okay."

"Just stay hidden," Mona told her,

"You all too," Sal said, looking around at the

rest of the stowaways. They looked the same way he'd imagined the lost boys in Peter Pan's Neverland might look—wild hair and smudged faces. Bright eyes and a crooked crown. True adventurers. "Hide in the caves."

"But don't pet the plants." Mona smirked. "Leave that to me."

"This is the day we've waited for," Frida said.

"Grandpa's good name
will be restored.
This last great fountain,
will at last be toast.
And we'll get Toot back.
I've missed him the most."

"We all have to work together," Sal reminded them. "Everything will happen fast. Let's trust each other."

He looked at Mona, and she nodded to him. Their truce was still in place.

Three of them headed back through the jungle, toward the raft to the boat and then to the mist to bring a villain closer.

And Sal, Frida, Sundae, Mama, and the others

waited—in this strange island's quiet—for everyone to return. For everything that would happen.

~~~

Desdemona's small yacht bobbed in the ocean. The boat had stopped working the other day, just when she had that ugly library ship in her sights.

"I'm tempted to let the boat sit here until they're finished," Stanley told the small squirrel in his study. "But we should get there too. In case they need us. Do you think you can fix it?"

With a chirp and a salute, the squirrel scrambled away to work.

Stanley looked out at the sea.

He had much on his mind.

Much more on his heart.

This strange adventure had started when he was a child. And it had changed his life in so many sad ways. He had lost his wife and his best friend over all of this. Then a daughter. And now his grandchildren were missing.

All of his grandchildren.

Was it too late to make anything right again?

"I can only try," he said softly. But how?

A flash of purple caught his eye out the window. He stood and looked and saw the tiniest ripple below.

The motor whirred again. And, very slowly, the boat began to move.

Minutes later the squirrel, dripping wet, joined Stanley back in the study. Stanley wrapped a tiny towel around the creature's shoulders. It rested a small, metal paw on the old man's hand.

"Thank you," Stanley said.

"The boat is moving!" Desdemona shouted from above. "Steer, Joffkins! That old man is trying to cheat us out of our treasure, and I won't let him. We are so close!"

She didn't even mention that her kids were missing, Stan realized. What kind of daughter had he raised?

"Not far to the meeting place!" Desdemona called out. "Then those wretched Problems will come get us and lead us to the treasure." She clapped her hands. "Everything is working out just like I knew it would."

Stan hoped that was not true. He would do what he had to do to make sure it wasn't.

⨯⨯⨯⨯

Arianna stood at the helm of the boat holding Toot. Augustus Snide stood beside her, eyes fixed on the mist ahead.

"Don't let the baby go," the old man said. His voice sounded thinner now and strained. He needed the water badly. "They might try something in the mist. He's our hostage until I have the water."

"And then I'm free," she reminded him.

"I'm a man of my word," he said.

It wasn't an especially warm day, but Ari felt sweat beading on her forehead. There was a tingly feeling in her throat she couldn't swallow down. Where were the Problims? Where was Sal? They wouldn't try anything, would they? Because Augustus was tricky and smart. He would disappear with Toot and the Problims would never see them again if they didn't play this exactly as he had requested.

A low *woooomp*,[14] and Toot pointed to the horizon. A ship full of children—with the scary Problim girl standing on the deck—burst through the mist.

From behind them, Ari saw a tiny yacht clunking toward them. Desdemona's boat, no doubt. "Gang's all here," she said softly.

---

14 **#35:** The Fart of the Four Winds: The flatulent rally of true adventure. Contains bold notes of dead fish in the ocean and chicken litter in a wide-open field.

Toot squealed. And clapped. And farted[15] again.

"I can't wait to get that wretch off my boat," Cheese Breath said through clenched teeth.

Arianna didn't notice the smell. She only noticed relief rolling over her like a warm ocean wave. Relief . . . what a weird feeling to have. The Problims hated her. Mona Problim had always looked ready to strangle her when they'd locked eyes. But still, she felt like everything would be okay if they were here. The Problim children would make it right again.

"And so it begins," Cheese Breath said. "Or so it ends, I guess I should say."

Ari heard what sounded like a low chuckle in his throat. Carrying Toot, she followed Augustus and climbed onto the library ship. And they sailed into the darkness, toward the island. Toward freedom. And toward the friend she'd betrayed.

---

15 **#45**: The Braveheart Fart: The toot used by Toot to summon his courage and drive fear into his enemies' hearts. Smells like moldy cheese and sweaty victory.

The Arrival

Sal waited at the rabbit-shaped cave between Sundae and Violet. Biscuit sat in front of them, keeping watch. Mama was hidden, because it was almost time. It all came down to this.

Sal pushed up the sleeves of his shirt, and his pale arms seemed extra bright in the light. He wished he hadn't left his jacket on the beach. How would he intimidate Cheese Breath without it?

Maybe it's good that he underestimates me, he thought. It's not like I can physically intimidate anybody. But I can sure as heck outthink them.

"I want this day to be over with," Violet said. "I don't like this part of the adventure."

Sal agreed.

Usually he would not advise wishing time away. Time was a really precious thing. It's not like you ever get it back. The time they actually had with Grandpa Problim, for example, was so short. Too short. But in this case, Violet had a point. He felt like they'd been watching the jungle for hours, waiting for the trees to rustle, for his siblings—and the villains—to walk into his sights. But every time he checked his watch, it seemed like only a few minutes had past. Time was a terrible prankster.

"They're coming," Violet said.

Sal felt an oddly warm wind. The trees rustled. There were voices.

Desdemona: "I hate mosquitos! Of all the horrible places for a fountain to be . . ."

Joffkins: "Violet!" He called again, "VIOLET!"

Violet sighed, a crackle through her mask. "He's so mad."

And then . . . a smell.[16]

"Tootykins!" Sundae said with a gasp.

Sal held his breath, not just because the toot was

---

16 **#211:** The Motto Fart: A flatulent trumpet of declaration embracing Toot's life philosophy: fart loudly and proudly and be brave and courageous.

vile. But because he was afraid he was dreaming.

The group emerged from the woods. Most of them looked dirty, sweaty, and haggard. Desdemona had leaves in her hair. Cheese Breath staggered as he walked. Sal hoped the mist had been especially horrible for him. Thea, Wendell, and Mona followed behind the raggedy group. And then there was Stan O'Pinion.

Sal's other grandfather.

Stan didn't look like Grandpa Problim. He had a different face shape. He was taller. But there was a gentleness around his eyes. He'd seen the Problims back on the Isle of St. Maria, Sal was sure of it now. But he had let them get away. The old man nodded at Sal, and Sal, unsure of what else to do, nodded back.

Toot Problim looked as dapper as ever, bow tie barely crooked. He was secure in the arms of Sal's former friend, Arianna.

At the sight of the baby, Sal smiled. And held his breath. He assumed Toot would turn loose some rancid fart of complete happiness. Instead, the baby waved at his big brother. And said, "Sal."

Sundae gasped. "That's his first word!"

Toot made grabby hands for his brother as he got

closer. Sal's throat felt thick with emotion now: not sadness, really. But absolute overwhelm. He reached for Toot.

"NO!" Cheese Breath said. "Hold the baby tight, girl. They get him when I get my water."

Sal felt heat rising to his face when he saw Ari. All along, she had been tricking him. It had felt so real, their friendship, but she had been using him to get to this place. To get to the fountain and help this terrible old man find what he wanted. A villain disguised as a friend was the worst villain of all, in his book.

That's what he told himself when she walked toward him and spoke. "Toot's okay. I won't let anybody hurt him. I promised."

"Your promises don't mean anything," he said, grabbing for his brother.

"No," Augustus shouted. "Not until we reach the fountain. Hold him until we get to the water, girl."

Toot tooted at his brother.[17] Sal nodded. And then the toddler folded his arms, ready for this

---

17 #201: The Empathizer: Means: I see you, I understand you, and I care about you. Smells like: sweaty armpits on a hot day.

miserable adventure to be over with. Such a bossy little prisoner. A little prisoner . . . who seemed to be very much in control. Sal had to fight to keep the smile off his face. The Problim children were together again, for now.

"The fountain of youth is in there," Sal said, pointing toward the dark mouth of the cave.

"Then lead me to it," Cheese Breath said through clenched teeth. "Your little friends can stay out here."

"I'm going in," Desdemona cried out. "Half the water. That was our agreement, Snide."

"There are some things I need to tell you all first," Sal said. He took a deep breath. "Before we take you there."

How could he work this?

Grandpa hadn't intended for this to happen. He'd made this island a riddle so Cheese Breath wouldn't find his way through. And now they'd made it easy, leading that old weirdo right to the fountain. Sal's mind was so full of ideas on how to actually smash this thing—and still save his brother—that he couldn't isolate one good thought and think it through.

"There are rules for going inside," Sal said.

The Problim children and their friends nodded in agreement.

"What rules?" Cheese Breath said, his voice hovering on a laugh.

"You have to follow us," Sal said. "Wendell is the only one who can lead us to the fountain. And you need to watch out for the plants. They're evil. They're as bad as you. They'll kill us, if they have to, to keep the fountain and the other plants safe."

Cheese Breath, Des, and Joffkins all stared at Sal as if he'd grown a second head. They thought he was lying. Some adults had no imagination whatsoever. But Stan O'Pinion looked at Sal nodding, as if he believed him.

"Time is ticking," Cheese Breath said.

Sal nodded to his brother. Wendell walked to the mouth of the cave, water witch extended in front of him like a sword. And the Problems—and the villains—descended into the dark.

30

The Fountain of Youth

hey moved slowly into the cave, darkness edging in around them. Sundae mumbled softly to herself, and the sunlight responded gently, illuminating the underground darkness in a dreamlike way.

"Proud of yourself?" Sal said to Ari as they descended. Anger bubbled in his chest like soda fizz. Some part of his heart tried to convince him, even now, to trust her. But how could he?

"Of course not," she said. "But we all do what we have to. Don't we?"

Toot tooted.[18]

---

18 **#78:** The Peace Keeper: A toot reminiscent of steamy cow poo in a sunlit field. Meant to be calming but is actually rancid.

Sal ignored him.

"For what it's worth," she said softly. "I am sorry. And I wish I could have been your friend. I wish it didn't have to be this way, but," she whispered, "it's the only way I can be free. Toot understands."

"Toot's nicer than I am," Sal told her.

"Not f-far now," Wendell said.

"You have a real family," Ari said. "I don't. Augustus doesn't care if I live or die. Do you know what it's like, to live with someone who doesn't actually care about you?"

"You could have lived with us," Sal said. "What's one more person? It would have been fine. You could have walked away and had a room at Number Seven Main Street." A place that felt very, very far away from this cold cave, he realized.

Ari was quiet for a moment. "I didn't know that."

Count to seven. Plant a seed instead. Open your heart. Trust people. That's what Mama would say. That's probably what she was thinking, if she was hiding in earshot right now. But for Ari? Ari who helped kidnap his brother? So *what* if she had some sappy, sad backstory? So what if she'd had a terrible life? She'd done a really bad thing—by choice! Still, the words nearly bubbling up out of his heart were

kind. He didn't want to say them. He fought them.
But the words came out anyway.

"You owe Cheese Breath nothing, Ari. He's a
scared old man. He lies and cheats to get what he
wants. But you don't have to be like him." He let out
a sad sigh. "You could still live with us if you want
to. Once all this is over. But you might have to go on
a few adventures."

She didn't speak, so he assumed she didn't care.
But then he heard the softest sob in the darkness.
When he looked to his side, when he saw the glint of
a tear on her face, his heart softened. Like spring dirt
when flowers are about to push through. That's the
problem with planting seeds, he decided. After you
spend so much time looking for the best in people, it
becomes natural. Easy. Even for an enemy who used
to be a friend.

"All r-right," Wendell said. "H-here we are."

The tunnel opened to a wide cavern, just like in
Grandpa's photo. The ceiling was so high that it felt
like a mile away. Sharp stalactites dripped down all
around them. They reminded Sal of teeth.

And there, in front of them, was the fountain of
youth. The fountain people had died trying to find.
The simple, small body of water so many people

would give their lives for even now. It looked like a silvery pool, like a melted puddle of tin. The center rippled gently, and the edges had an unusual sheen. Almost a reddish hue.

Plants stood around the fountain like soldiers. Some were small ankle-biters clustered around the sides. But a few plants were tall as trees, stretching toward the sharp ceiling with the same, sinister alligator-shaped heads as the plants in the inn. Cave Bulbs, technically. Just huge ones. These looked a lot like large versions of Mona's Venus flytraps. Except Sal knew they ate far more than flies. . . .

The air was thick and smelled like sulphur and water (kind of like a #112,[19] Sal thought offhandedly.)

"Hand me the jars, girl," Cheese Breath ordered. "And keep the baby close."

The Problim children looked to Sal. What to do now? How to destroy the fountain before Cheese Breath got what he wanted and left?

Could Sal . . . reason with a villain?

Desdemona was fishing through a bag of her own. "I brought containers too," she said. "And I

---

19 **#112**: The Alphatoot: First created when Sundae tried to teach Toot his ABCs, and often tooted to the tune of the song. Smells like sulphur and lucky socks.

want to take pictures. . . ."

Carly-Rue grabbed her mom's wrist. She glared at her. "No."

Desdemona's eyebrows rose. "Excuse me?"

"Listen to her," Stan said, laying a hand on her shoulder. Desdemona shoved them both away, and walked toward the water.

"You know it makes you evil, right?" Sal said to both of them. His voice hovered on a yell. He would beg, if he had to. "I know Cheese Breath knows. You've felt it, surely. That water makes you vicious and violent. It doesn't heal anything. And it drowns out the good stuff."

"I am alive though, young Mr. Problim," Cheese Breath said, opening the jar Ari gave him. "That's better than your grandfather."

Sorrow pierced Sal's heart like an arrow. Once he would have done anything to avoid sadness. This is when opening his heart was painful. But way more often, he believed having a tender heart was good. Better than good.

"I don't think so," Sal said, his voice wavering. "The only thing he was afraid of was not living a life of love. Of not living a life of adventure. But he did both those things."

"Tell yourself what you must," Cheese Breath said. "But I could show you what it's like to live this way, you know. You could stay alive forever, Sal. So could your family. Think about that—you would never lose someone you love again. You could live on this island! Nobody would bother you. No more friends would betray you."

Sal felt Ari flinch beside him.

"No one would try to separate you," Cheese Breath added.

It sounded blissful, a little bit. But Sal knew the reality of that decision: the water would make them cruel. Would make them fight, hurt each other, grow bitter and violent. The cost was too high. "No," Sal said.

"What about the little bubble girl?" Cheese Breath asked. "Does she want to live life behind a mask for the rest of her life? Never smell the fresh air?"

"She's perfect the way she is," Joffkins snarled. He'd been standing directly behind Violet; he hadn't taken his eyes off her since they'd been reunited. But now, Joffkins rounded to stand beside her. He looked angry and protective. But Violet O'Pinion wasn't a girl who needed protecting. She took her dad's hand and looked Cheese Breath in the eye.

"I do smell the air," Violet said, with a shrug. "Just in a different way. I'm happy being me. This version of me. Sometimes things that sound too good to be true . . . well, they are."

Sal looked at Ari. She'd moved closer to him. She was steps away, and Toot's little hand was on her face like he was comforting her. That little traitor. And then, so softly, Toot puffed a #133.[20]

"Trust me," Sal whispered to Mona, to Wendell, and to Thea. "Please. Just trust me."

"Trust him," Stan said softly. The old man had moved quietly to stand behind the Problems. They all turned to look at him, surprised. "I wanted it to save someone I loved," Stan said. "Frank kept it from me because he knew what it could do. Do not drink it. Please."

"Suit yourselves," said Cheese Breath. "I have a date with eternity."

He staggered toward the water with his open jar. So did Desdemona.

And an orange flame jumped from her hiding

---

20 #133: The Brotherly Love: A toot puffed on the occasion when Toot wants one of his brothers, or will wait for one of his brothers, or just wants to share his love for his brothers. Smells a bit like grilled cheese, a bit like garlic, and a lot like sports gear forgotten in a plastic bag for a week.

place and grabbed Cheese Breath's foot. He stumbled. "Tricks, eh? I warned you. . . ."

A silvery-purple bolt of light zoomed through the cave next, landing on Cheese Breath's head. He batted at the mechanical squirrel, shouting.

"Ari," Sal said, reaching for her. "Give me Toot. And go, if you want. But give him to me."

She edged a little closer to him.

"Don't do it, girl!" Cheese Breath shouted. "Bring the baby to me! Now!"

Ari looked into Sal's eyes. He didn't know what she saw there, but something made her lift her arms and pass Toot to him. He seemed heavier than he did a few days ago. Or maybe just the weight of him was so comforting that it shocked him a little bit. Sal kissed the baby's forehead. And Toot nuzzled into Sal's neck, happy to be home.

"Get out," Sal told her. "Everybody out!" Sal shouted. "We're going to destroy the fountain whether or not he leaves."

"Not without my mom!" Carly-Rue yelled.

"I'll get her," Mama Problim shouted. She'd come out of her hiding place and looked ready to fight something.

Cheese Breath chuckled, "Did you bring Mommy

to do the job for you, little Problims?"

Sal glanced at Mama, but before he could speak she lifted a hand. "I won't interfere. Just let me get everyone out."

"Mina . . . ," Stanley O'Pinion's voice sounded like it had been raked over gravel. "Mina?"

"Dad!" Mama Problim said, hugging him quickly. "Let's all get out. You too, Des."

Des, standing knee-deep in the fountain's pool, glared. "No," she spat the word. "I have a destiny. Same as you. I can do remarkable things, the same as you. Go back to your hiding spot, Mina. Hide and let your children take care of you."

"We can continue this family reunion outside, if you'd like," Cheese Breath said, holding up a jar full of silver liquid. "I got what I need." He laughed and lifted the water to his mouth to drink.

"Don't!" Sal shouted.

As the jar touched the old man's lips, Stanley O'Pinion stepped in front of Cheese Breath, grabbed the water and flung it to the ground. It landed with a shattering smash. Violet snatched Stanley's hand and pulled him away, just as Cheese Breath lunged for him. With a growl, Cheese Breath hit the ground. On his forearms, he soldier-crawled back to the water and brought it to his mouth in handfuls of silver.

"NO!" Sal shouted, his hands balling into fists.

Desdemona filled her own jar and tried to put on a lid with shaky hands.

"Are you kidding me?" Mama Problim yelled at her sister. She was as fed up as Sal got with Mona. Desdemona ignored her.

"Everybody out now," Sal said to his family. "Please! We'll bring it down from the outside."

Then Sal closed his eyes. He unlocked the earth. He imagined the cave like a giant puzzle. And he removed one piece. . . .

A stalactite fell from the ceiling, splashing into the center of the pool.

"The cave's coming down," Sal said, glaring at Cheese Breath. "This is your last chance to leave."

But the old man didn't listen. He crawled to the edge of the pool, scooping more eternal water into his hands. Splashing it onto his face.

"Mom!" Carly-Rue shouted, "Let's go! Please!"

"NOT YET!" Desdemona shouted, as she filled a second jar full of the water. Her hands trembled, but she didn't even look up.

Will picked up Carly-Rue, despite her protests, and ran toward the opening of the cave. LeeLee,

Alabama, and Noah followed.

"Let's go," Sundae said, taking Alex's hand and running for the sunlight. Wendell, Thea, and Mona followed her.

Violet pulled at Stanley's hand. "We have to go, Grandpa!" she said.

He smiled down at her. "Take your little dog and go. I'm right behind you."

"Go," Sal said to his mama. She was holding Toot on her hip.

"I'll be right out," Sal said. "I promise." She ran away. Everybody was out now except Sal, Stanley, Desdemona, and Violet.

Another stalactite smashed to the ground, stabbing the dirt beside Sal's shoe. Was the cave trying to protect itself? Protect its secret? Sal looked into Violet's eyes. "You go. I'll get your grandpa out. Our grandpa, I mean."

With tears streaming down her face, she stumbled toward the light.

Sal turned his head just in time to see Stanley O'Pinion walk up behind Cheese Breath—still halfway submerged in the pool—and lifted his boot. Ready to try and fight him. Ready to do whatever he had to to keep him here in the cave. But there was a problem . . . Stan O'Pinion was old. Cheese Breath, though older, had just guzzled enchanted water.

With a snarl, Cheese Breath stood in a whirl and knocked Stan O'Pinion to the edge of the pool. A clatter of rocks fell from overhead, crashing into the ground.

"Go on, Sal," Stanley yelled, pushing himself up on shaky arms. "Get out!"

"Come with me, Gr—" Sal swallowed hard. "Grandpa. Come with me!"

A shimmer of tears pooled in Stanley's eyes as he looked up at Sal and offered a tired smile.

Sal reached to help him. But Stan lifted his hand as if to say: stop.

"Leave me," Stanley begged. "I'll keep him here. I just want your family . . . my family . . . to be safe."

Sal felt the strangest tug at the corners of his heart. Stanley O'Pinion, the Big Bad, was willing to die for him. Maybe he had been a villain, for a while. But to die for someone you love . . . that's something only a hero does.

Cheese Breath hovered over the old man and lifted his boot. Sal lifted the big pliers he'd been carrying, the last remnant of his jacket and flung them like a frisbee, knocking into one of the giant plants.

Cheese Breath paused and stared at Sal, gloating. "You missed."

Sal smiled. "No, I didn't. I wasn't aiming at you."

The plant began to shiver, then stretch. Cheese Breath turned to look at it. "What is this?" he asked.

The tall stem of the plant coiled into a spiral shape, then tipped its flowery head toward Cheese Breath. The flower opened to show rows of teeth just before it snapped down around Augustus Snide . . . swallowing him whole.

Another stalactite crashed to the ground.

"Come on," Sal said, reaching for his grandfather. His grandfather . . . wow. He draped Stanley's arm around his shoulders, hooked his own arm around the old man's thin waist, and helped him up through the tunnel.

Long, green vines reached for them, lashed at them like emerald whips.

"Sal!" someone called from behind him. Desdemona. The plant had caught her, pulling her backward, chomping as one long vine pulled her closer to its mouth. "Please!" she said. "Help me!"

If you had asked Sal Problem a few weeks ago how this scene would make him feel, he might have thought it would make him feel great. But there was nothing great, he realized, in seeing anyone suffer. There was nothing great about the thought of Carly-Rue not having a mom. Even if her mom was kind of a jerk.

Sal reached for the axe on his jacket . . . then remembered he wasn't wearing his jacket.

"Mom!" Carly-Rue O'Pinion shouted, running past him in a blur. She held the axe Sal had given her high in her hand. She aimed and threw—tossing the axe over Desdemona's head . . . and missing the green vine by an inch. Then, without hesitation, she pulled off her sparkly tiara and flung it with a mighty scream. The crown lodged in the plant's mouth, and Des scrambled to her feet. The jars she'd held so tightly crashed to the ground in the chaos.

Carly-Rue latched on to her mom's hand and ran alongside Sal and Stan. They all burst out of the cave, into the crowd of Problims, O'Pinions, and stowaways waiting to help them.

Desdemona staggered away toward the woods, as far as she could get from the cave. Stanley and Mina Problim stood ten feet behind the Problim children. Close enough to help, if needed. But far enough to give them space to do what they were meant to do.

"Let's finish it!" Sal shouted to his siblings. And they ran to him, standing side by side, eyes closed. They joined hands.

The earth began to rumble.

Then growl.

One rock-formation bunny ear came crashing down. Then the next. A wild wind howled through the woods, spinning up the dirt all around them.

Sal imagined the earth unlocking its doors, showing him every secret, opening up every single hiding place. He didn't watch the cave smash . . . but he heard it. And he felt it. And on the backs of his eyelids, he saw his siblings. They clicked past his imagination like a slideshow:

Mona staring into the mist, daring it to try and scare her . . .

Toot on the sea, arms crossed, a hero, not a captive . . .

Wendell commanding the ocean . . .

Thea unlocking doors, turning her face to the light, blooming . . .

Frida throwing beams of fire from her hands . . .

Sundae speaking sunlight into every dark corner.

And him too. No jacket this time. It had never been what made him magical. Sal spoke to the earth, and the earth spoke back.

A wild wind whipped around the seven, tossing their hair, pitching them forward, but they never let go.

They would never let go.

"Just like all those years ago," Stan said. "Such magic . . ."

And just when Sal thought he couldn't concentrate any harder, the rocks burst. The cave imploded into a ball of fire, singeing the stone. Collapsing on itself. Blocking the entrance. Barring the fountain from visitors forever.

Sal opened his eyes to realize he was sitting on the ground, breathing heavily. His siblings were there too, in a line beside him. Toot had crawled into his mama's arms.

For a while, there was silence. Then the sound of Desdemona sobbing, softly. And then, peace.

31

A Feud Forgotten

As the sun sank lower over the island, a new truce was called. The feud was over. The Problem children, the O'Pinion children, and all of their friends had decided it was past time for this. "We can't tell you what to do," Sal said to Desdemona, Joffkins, and Stan. And his mother too. "But it stops here. It stops with us."

Mona and Carly-Rue, who stood with their arms around each other, nodded. So did Will, Thea, Violet, Sundae, and Toot.

"Good," Stanley O'Pinion said. Violet flew at him, hugging him tight. "I can't take back the years I missed," he told the Problem children. "But I'm your grandfather too starting now. Today. If you'll let me be."

The Problim children didn't need to think about it. They swarmed him, hugging him tight. Sal had thought his days of having a grandfather were over, but they weren't. No, Stan wasn't Frank. But Violet had told him that he was a great grandpa. And he trusted her.

Stan reached out for one more person as they huddled together—their mom. She flew into his embrace too, for the first time in years. Funny, Sal thought, how smashing a treasure had led them to something better. Something that felt more real.

"Ari," Sal said. She looked up suddenly. She'd been standing alone, arms crossed, eyes on the ground. He stretched out his hand.

But she shook her head. "I should go. Have an adventure or something."

"Okay," Sal said. "But whether you go or stay, if you want a family you've got one."

And then she was in their huddle too. As much as Sal hated hugs, this all felt okay somehow.

"Des?" Mama Problim said, reaching for her. "It's over now. Isn't it?"

Desdemona stood quietly, watching. She didn't

join the huddle. She didn't speak. She simply walked away, through the woods, back toward the ship. "Come on, Joffkins," she said.

But Joffkins reached for his daughter's hand. "I'll ride with Violet. We have a lot to talk about."

"I agree," Violet said, with a smile.

The rest of them stopped only once on the way back to the shore, to drink from a spring that was not enchanted. Other than the fact that it made them less thirsty, which was a miracle in itself. While the children drank from it, and splashed their faces, and wiped the debris from their arms, Sal jogged up to the top of a flowery hill.

Maybe he should come back and explore someday. There were plants up here he had never seen before. Never even imagined. Trees dangled with flowery vines. Sunlight filtered through leafy branches, making pretty patterns all across the grass. Even the wind blew sweeter here. It all made him feel so suddenly joyful. So happy. Like he was home.

Like a thin place . . . the thing Grammy Payne had told him about back on the Isle of St. Maria. She'd said this island was full of thin places.

A thin place is a little pocket in our world that feels so beautiful, so special . . . you can see or feel a glimpse of the world beyond this one when you come upon it. . . .

Quickly, before anybody would miss him, Sal Problim decided to do one final experiment on the Island in the Stars.

32

Thin Places

Sal climbed to the top of a grassy hill. Surrounded by gentle (not miserable) mist rising from the ground, and by whispering trees, he was hidden from everyone (as far as he knew). But something about this place made him feel surrounded by a strange, new energy.

"Sal?" Mona called. "What are you doing up there?"

"Just a minute," Sal hollered to his sister. He ran forward, finding a bright, warm patch of sunlight to stand in. He didn't like sunshine usually. But this was different. Special. Otherworldly, almost.

Sal reached into his pocket and grabbed the vial

holding the last Wishbloom.

"You're being ridiculous," he said to himself, as he gently pulled the flower free from the glass. "So stupid." He held it up, near his mouth. And he made a wish:

"I wish I could tell Grandpa Problim I love him again."

The leaves caught his words and rolled them into a whistle. And the glitter on the last petal swirled up into the air. This time, the glitter-dust didn't fall on Sal's face, like it had back in the Swampy Woods. This time, the dust spun up and stretched out like a sparkly wave.

And then it stuck . . . to something.

It looked like an invisible screen, just a few feet in front of Sal's face. The glitter-dust clung to it, sparkling. And past that screen, as if Sal was watching through a blurry window, the world looked different. The hills were bright with colors he'd never seen before. But he could still feel the warm wind of that place. And he could see shadows of people. Blurry images just beyond recognition.

One shadow, in particular, didn't have to be refined for him to know who it was. Moving toward him was the shadow of an old man. The old man paused, standing just beyond that strange screen. He held up a shadowy hand. Behind him, the silhouette of a dog pounced around playfully.

"Nova?!" Will O'Pinion jogged up the hill. He stood behind Sal in shock. "What? . . . Whoa!"

"You see it?" Sal asked.

"I don't just see it," Will said. "I know that dog! I know this sounds crazy, dude, but . . . that's her. . . ." Will swallowed hard. "I would know her anywhere. What is this?" Will stared up at the shimmering screen in front of them.

"The G-Great F-Forever," Wendell Problim said. Sal hadn't even heard his brother walk up behind him. He glanced back to see all of the Problim children there.

"S-Sal found a thin p-place," Wendell said. "But how are w-we s-seeing it?!"

Toot groaned from Sundae's arms, reaching for Sal. So Sal took him, hoisting him high on his hip.

Toot waved at the shadow man. The man waved back.

Frida appeared beside Sal then, glowing, beaming. Shining like a tiny fire-star.

"Wishblooms," Sal said, stretching his fingers toward the screen. "Is that . . . him?"

Grandpa. Sal could almost—barely—make out the smile on the old man's face. Sal felt like he'd drunk a bottle of Bloomfizz even though his feet were firmly on the ground. He didn't know how long a window into a thin place lasted. But he knew this was real. It was unexplainable. And it was also real.

"Yeah," Thea said, her voice as soft as a secret. "That's him."

"I love you," Sal said bravely and loudly. And he realized then—deep in the truest part of his soul— that those were the bravest three words in the world. Because to love a person—or a pet—means you've opened your heart to a whole world of hurt. Life is dangerous. And if you love, Sal knew, eventually your heart would be broken over something. Or someone, more likely.

Oh, but it was worth it. Memories with Grandpa Problim clicked like a slideshow through Sal's mind. And though he heard no words, he saw the shadow-man—his grandfather, somewhere else, somewhere good—stretch out his hand toward him. Like they were almost touching. Like they would touch again someday. Sal felt the words in his heart as strongly as he'd ever felt words spoken:

I love you too, Sal Problim. Lasso the stars, sweet boy.

Sal felt two gentle hands rest on his shoulders, and looked up to see his other grandpa standing behind him. Stan watched the thin place, teary-eyed. He lifted his hand, waving to his friend. "I'll take care of them," he promised softly. "I'm sorry."

The Problim children all stood in a row with their mom and grandpa, watching—for a second—the shadowy lands beyond the thin place. As the sun sunk lower, the image began to fade—like an old TV getting fuzzy, ebbing away to darkness. The shadow-dog pounced away with a happy *YAP!*, running off into valleys and hills. And finally, the shadow-man turned to follow her.

There are things in this world that cannot be explained, Sal Problim decided. He said this as a man of science. A man of wonder. A man of magic.

"Problims!" someone shouted, followed by the sound of heavy boots running through the jungle. "Mina! Sundae? Kids?"

Papa Problim stomped out of the foliage, sweaty-faced and smiling. And then Mama was looking at him, hands on her hips. "What?" she asked.

"I'm here to rescue you!" he shouted.

Mama looked back at the kids and winked. And they all erupted in laughter so sweet and freeing. The kind that had been building up for months.

33

Return of the Seven (Again)

The mechanical squirrel chattered madly from the crow's nest as the library boat neared the harbor of Lost Cove. Desdemona had refused to board, insisting on taking the yacht back alone. But the rest of the crew—now even larger than before—stood together on the top deck of the ship. Sal couldn't wait to see the town again. He knew its streets and spires and docks. He knew the shortcut to the donut shops and seven different routes to get home to Number Seven Main Street. He missed that house. He would get to sleep in his own bed tonight. Or in his sleeping bag in the backyard. Or in the strong arm of the oak tree. It didn't matter—he was nearly home!

And when he woke up tomorrow morning, Wendell would be making pancakes for everyone. For all seven Problim children. For the Problim parents. For Ichabod. And the stowaways. And Ari, maybe.

"Are you sure," she asked, standing beside him, "that I can stay with you?"

"Yes," he said. "Just don't kidnap any more of my siblings."

He smiled at her, and she smiled back. The thought of showing her Lost Cove made him very happy.

The Problim family was finally together.

Sal glanced over at his parents standing against the rail. Papa's arms were locked loosely around Mama's waist. They're like sequoia trees, he decided. Strong and steady because they're close—their roots connect, but they stand tall on their own. The two of them looked ahead with peaceful expressions on their faces.

Peace for now, at least. They were true adventurers, Sal knew. The Problim parents wouldn't stay put for long. They were happiest out in the world, exploring. Grandpa O'Pinion had offered to be their guardian next time the parents were out of the country. (He seemed particularly excited about taking a ride on the human catapult.) Sal wondered if he'd feel the same as his parents someday, that same ache for adventure. If he felt it a little bit already. If it was time for them all to go together, maybe. (Including Ari. She was already a proven adventurer too.)

Sal meandered closer to his parents, hands in his pockets. He missed the sound of his tools, the way they clattered like soft rain on the rooftops. Maybe he'd needed to let the old jacket go. To see that he was capable of plenty without it. But he couldn't wait to get home and make a new one. "So," he began, "if Mama was helping Grandpa Problim get this whole thing started . . . does that mean you know how the bungalow imploded?"

Mama glanced at Mona.

Mona smiled. "I received a letter in the mail with a prompt, shall we say. I didn't know much more than that."

"I didn't tell her to kaboom the house," Mama said. "Not in those words. But that was a creative way to interpret my note."

"The watch came from an anonymous sender," Mona said with a shrug. "I've had it since the Swampy

Woods. I was instructed to press the button on the watch in a time of deepest distress. I figured being lost at sea was sufficiently distressful."

"Where'd the bird go?" Sal asked, suddenly curious.

Mona shrugged. "Sundae said it zoomed out the window while she and Alex were guarding the boat. Who knows where it landed. Grandpa's creatures have minds of their own."

"Now we can all truly settle in at home," Sundae said. "School starts in a few weeks in Lost Cove."

Sal grimaced. "We're not trying real school, are we?"

"Not unless you want to," Mama Problim said. "Or . . ." She looked back at Papa. "Can I tell them now?"

Papa smiled. "Sure. Why not?"

"Tell us what?" Sal asked, looking between them suspiciously.

Mama smiled, glancing around at all of them. "Or you could take your studies abroad. Papa and I are taking a sabbatical from Andorra. We've got a lead on another treasure in another country. And it's something dazzling."

"A treasure beyond measure?" asked the fox, pouncing up beside Sal.

Mama nodded. "The sword of a king," she whispered. "The last relic of a land called Camelot."

"K-King A-Arthur's s-sword?" Wendell shouted excitedly. "But it's a m-myth."

"Is it?" Mom asked. "We've been looking for it for a while now. And we have an idea where it could be. We could use a great team of seekers to help us. It will be perilous, of course. But . . . how do you feel about a family trip to England?"

Sal looked back at his siblings, surprised to find they were all watching to see his response. None of them were shy about making up their own minds. But for some reason, they wanted him to go first. Even Mona, to his great shock.

"Only if we all go," Sal said. "Including Ari. For as long as we can, let's stick together."

Ari, who was holding Toot on her hip, smiled.

Mona nodded. "Agreed."

"Really?" Sal asked. "You're agreeing with me?"

She waved him off. "I agree with you when you say smart things. Which isn't very often. But it does happen."

"Together's my favorite place to be," Thea said. "I agree too. Shall we vote?"

The vote was unanimous, all the way down the aisle.

"And you're welcome to come too, Violet," Mama Problim said. "If you'd like to. . . ."

Violet sighed, her mask crackling happily. "I really should talk to my dad. First, I need to make sure I'm not in trouble for this adventure. Then I'll convince him I can have another one."

Stan rested a comforting hand on his granddaughter's helmet. "I can help with that."

"LAND AHEAD!" shouted the fox.

"Lost Cove is nigh!
Watch for rocks,
or we'll all die."

"So bleak, Frida," Mona said, with a smirk. "I like it."

"FRIDA!" Violet shouted, waving up to the crow's nest. "I see her!"

"I see her when I squint," Noah said excitedly. "I can't wait to see her for real. I'm close, Frida!"

The fox smiled and saluted them both.

Mona elbowed Sal. "So do you have a plan in place for when we land? You know Desdemona the Totally Vile will have police waiting to whisk us away. We broke into her house, for one. She didn't get any water, for two."

"But we saved her life," Sal said.

Thea shrugged. "Doesn't matter to her. She'll probably have the Society for the Protection of Unwanted Children here again too. And Miss Sanchez will be mad because the library boat is looking rough and—"

They all went quiet at the sight in front of them. When the boat crested a last tall wave and the harbor became clear, they realized an angry mob had not gathered on the shores of Lost Cove. Instead, the entire town had shown up to cheer their return.

WELCOME HOME, PROBLEMS!

The banner was so bold and so big, they could see it all the way from the deck of the ship.

Wild cheers echoed against the cliffs and the sea. As the ship got closer, they could make out the faces of their friends. Mayor Wordhouse stood clapping, beaming. Melody Larson, her dog Xena, and kids they barely knew were waving from the shore. Even

the MOOS (the town's esteemed Mansion Own-
ers Observation Society—ladies who'd originally
despised the Problims) were applauding! Desdemona
stood on the pier as well. She was not cheering.

When the Problims—and their stowaways—
disembarked, they were crowded with hugs and
high fives.

Miriam Sanchez touched Wendell's shoulder.
"How did my ship do?"

"P-perfect," Wendell said. "She's a f-fine vessel."

Miriam beamed. "Come by the library whenever
you want. You can help me take care of it if you like.
Get it ready for the next brave soul who needs its
help."

"I would l-love th-th—" Wendell was suddenly
picked up off the ground, sandwiched in a hug
between the Donut sisters.

"We missed you, buddy!" Bertha hollered.

"More than you'll ever know," Dorothy added.

Thea sighed in happiness, watching how her
brother was loved. Then someone rested a hand on
her back, and she swirled into the welcoming arms
of Midge Lodestar, her mentor and life coach. "I
want you to write all about this," Midge said. "You
have so many stories to tell, Thea Problim."

Alex took Sundae's hand and led her to his family to introduce her. Formally.

Carly-Rue slipped her arm through Mona's (and Mona actually let her). They ran to a group of friends they'd made in the pageant.

Toot was happy in his mama's arms and was soon being loved on by all the moms and dads in the cove. He let out a celebratory toot.[21] And then another.[22]

Violet O'Pinion walked down the gangplank holding her father's hand. Her eyes were alight with wonder and adventure, the same as always. Biscuit pranced happily beside her. Looking back at Sal, she waved. And it was as if he could see an outline of wings behind her, even though she wasn't wearing them. Violet O'Pinion was a girl destined to have a lifetime of wonderful adventures. And so was her faithful, fuzzy little dog. (Sal could have sworn Biscuit winked at him as he thought this.) Ari walked on Violet's other side. Sal watched as Violet looped her arm through Ari's, telling her stories or secrets

---

21 #124: The Joyful, Joyful: Simple flatulence of happiness. Smells like a week-old bouquet of daisies.

22 #211: The Motto Fart: A flatulent trumpet of declaration embracing Toot's life philosophy: fart loudly and proudly and be brave and courageous.

or something—he didn't know what—that made Ari's shoulders settle. And a smile crossed her face.

Only Frida and Sal stayed on the ship a bit longer.

"If ever there's a day
when I'm not in your sights,
just know that I love you.
And that I'm all right," Frida said. And added,
*   in a whisper:*
"Maybe I'll disappear once and for all
*   someday."*

Sal shook his head. "You won't. You're never invisible to people who love you. And we do. Stick with me."

He had an idea.

"This is my sister, Frida," Sal said, ushering her through the crowd. He saw the confusion in people's eyes. "I know, she's hard to see at first. But if you concentrate on her . . . you'll see her. And once you see her and realize how cool she is, you'll wonder how you ever missed her."

The fox looked up into her big brother's eyes, with tiny tears twinkling in the corners of her own. "You are the most wonderful big brother," she said to him.

And he watched her shoulders pick up and her smile stretch wide. She bloomed, just like that.

~

Before Sal fell asleep that night, he snuck up to the roof. The night air felt strange on his bare arms. Strange, but okay. Maybe he would make another jacket someday, but it really would just be for gardening. He didn't need a coat to protect his heart. And he could plant seeds of possibility whether or not he had packets of marigolds in his pocket. For now, the only tool he needed was a pen. He pulled one from his pocket and opened up to a blank page in one of his old scientific notebooks.

I AM SAL PROBLIM.
I AM AN ADVENTURER.
A SCIENTIST. A GOOD BROTHER...
AND A SO-SO BABYSITTER.
I DRIVE PIRATE SHIPS.
I SPEAK TO PLANTS. I SET THE
WORLD TO BLOOMING.

He paused, remembering the shadow on the starry island. Remembering the gentle face he'd looked into for many years. The man who had taught him how to garden. Who sang silly songs with him while the sun set. Who had taught him that the world was full of wonder. Who he missed, and would always miss, but . . . who was a part of him in a way that could never be changed.

> I LOVE—AND TRUST—
> EVEN IF IT HURTS.

"I lasso the stars," Sal whispered and he imagined his breath floating up and up. Like glitter dust from a Wishbloom. An "I love you" soaring past the heavens and into the stars where it would stay and sparkle, for the rest of time.

The Squirrel's Reprieve

Outside House Number Seven, a weary mechanical squirrel climbed into its hometree. It nestled into its favorite nook and pulled the blanket Sundae Problem had made for it around its shoulders.

And then—delight!

The squirrel was elated to find a banner woven just for it by a bunch of sentimental circus spiders.

WELKOM HOM, SQGIRL!

(Not all spiders are good spellers, the squirrel knew. But it was a kind effort!)

Just as the squirrel was about to close its metal eyelids, the sweetest whistle floated down through the branches. The whistle stretched out and became a familiar tune, a song the squirrel knew by heart. It had heard it for the first time years ago. Back when it came alive in Frank Problim's workshop. When it saw the man's gentle blue eyes and heard him say, "Oh! Hello, friend!" Frank had been singing a song about the days of the week. He loved that song.

"I'll make you a friend to sing it with someday," Frank had told the squirrel. "So that if I ever go, you'll always have someone to sing with."

The squirrel knew Frank had meant well. The old man had wanted to create a friend for the squirrel. He simply didn't have enough time.

But now, that same song was chirped by a mechanical bird, perched in the limbs above.

A friend. Dear old Frank *had* made a friend for the squirrel, just as he had promised.

The squirrel climbed the branches and sat down beside the bird. It wrapped the small blanket around them both. Robo-creatures can't get cold, but that doesn't matter. A blanket is one of the best gifts you can give, especially to a friend. Squirrels know this. So it shared, and listened happily, as their mechanical hearts began to *tick-tock-whir* in perfect harmony.

As the lights faded on House Number Seven, the squirrel chattered at the bird, telling it a story. A story about the seven Problim children on the day they stumbled into Lost Cove. Maybe they are cursed, someone had said. No, someone else had argued, they're worse than that—they're magic.

That was the truth, of course. A good truth, not a terrible one.

elles

Yes, the squirrel told the bird, the Problim children are full of magic.

All children are.

Acknowledgments

For this final, stormy adventure I got to take with the Problems, I am extra grateful to the following folks: Maria Barbo (my friend and editor who reminded me to stay playful, joyful, and wild), Stephanie Guerdan (a wondrous reader and brainstormer), Jenny Moles (copy-editing genius), Katherine Tegen (Queen of Troublemakers), and the entire magical marketing, library, and sales team at HarperCollins/Katherine Tegen. I am also indebted to Suzie Townsend, my brilliant agent, who has ridden many metaphorical human catapults with me during my publishing journey. Abundant hugs (and toots) are also owed to Dani Segalbaum, Pouya Shahbazian, and my entire New Leaf family.

I am grateful to my actual family for loving me and making me laugh. They're the reason I wanted to write about a big, weird family in the first place. Justin, especially, has my whole heart and lets me bounce ideas off his marvelous brain even in the middle of the night when he would probably rather be sleeping. I'm grateful to God for all of these people, and for the way they spin my heart.

I'm grateful to booksellers, librarians, teachers, book bloggers, and social media wizards who've shared the Problim Children and helped them find new homes in readers' hearts. Highest fives to my hometown indie, Starline Books, for their endless support.

I didn't know if I should write this next part, because it is sad. You can skip this paragraph if you'd like. But I have learned that sadness often coexists with every feeling, especially gratitude. And I believe that it's important to share all your feelings with people you care about. So, that said, this is the final book that I wrote with my sweet dog, Biscuit, beside me. Losing her has been a most terrible grief. She was a precious friend to me and a magical little creature. Like Will's dog, Nova, I love to imagine Biscuit running, barking, and chasing butterflies in the Great Beyond. She made me dream bigger and want to be a better person. I miss her. I love her. And I am thankful she's in the pages of this book.

And my word, dear reader, I am grateful for you. Thank you for following the Problim children to the end of their journey. Thank you for wearing fox ears, like Frida, at school visits and sending me drawings of Ichabod and brainstorming ideas for new toot-smells. Whether or not you have a big family full of siblings to remind you, I hope you know that you are **not** invisible. You are loved, you are awesome, and you are destined for marvelous things. It is an honor to write stories for you.